Couples 101

Couples 101

A'ndrea J. Wilson

The Wife 101 Series ❧ Book 3

Divine Garden Press

Published by Divine Garden Press, LLC
PO Box 371
Soperton, GA 30457

ISBN-13: 978-0615829845
ISBN-10: 0615829848
Library of Congress Control Number: 2013941982
Cover Design & Interior Layout: A'ndrea J. Wilson
Cover Photography: The Snappy Diva (www.thesnappydiva.com)

Scripture taken from THE AMPLIFIED BIBLE, Old Testament copyright © 1065, 1987 by the Zondervan Corporation. The Amplified New Testament copyright © 1958, 1987 by The Lockman Foundation. Used by permission.

Scripture taken from The Holy Bible, King James Version, Old and New Testament copyright © 1984, 1977 by Thomas Nelson, Inc.

Lyrics used from Tis So Sweet. Copyright ©1882 by Louisa M. R. Stead.

The Awareness Wheel. Copyright © 1990 by Interpersonal Communication Programs, Inc.

"LOVE TAKES OFF MASKS THAT WE FEAR WE CANNOT LIVE WITHOUT AND KNOW WE CANNOT LIVE WITHIN."

JAMES BALDWIN

Lesson 1: There is a Time

To everything there is a season and a time. (Ecclesiastes 3:1)

Dr. Wilson

I loved being a psychologist, but even the best therapists in the world need counseling. We also need vacations. At that moment, God was somewhat granting and rejecting my plea for downtime. I was sitting on a flight from Rochester, New York to Miami, Florida to facilitate couples therapy sessions for an Atlanta-based church's marriage retreat. I was originally supposed to help out with this retreat in August; however, due to some scheduling conflicts at the host church, the retreat had been pushed back to the first week in November.

I sighed as I realized that I was sitting in between two forces that I couldn't control. To my left was the airplane window, clearly displaying frigid snow flurries which seemed to dance and swirl their way from the sky down to the tar-covered runway concrete. I despised snow, which Rochester was famous for; therefore, I appreciated the idea of the tropical getaway. I would have moved away from this city a long time ago had it not been for the force to my right, my husband, Lemuel, who was referred to as Lem. Born and raised in Upstate, New York, Lem was comfortable staying close to everything and everyone he knew. I was also from the area, but beyond ready for a change. My career as a psychologist and speaker afforded me the luxury of traveling often and experiencing new people and places. Meanwhile, Lem's career in construction as a home builder kept him local most of the time, which was exactly where he wanted to be.

For the most part, our marriage was good, and I was glad to have a loving spouse. He understood how important it was for me to have a healthy marriage since I was considered a relationship expert. I wasn't so sure that I was actually an expert in marriage or even dating, but I was passionate about the topic and willing to learn and grow in it. To demonstrate his support, Lem traveled with me occasionally to various marriage engagements, especially ones such as this that would provide him a free stay on Miami's South Beach for an entire week.

Seven days. I had seven days to work with four couples that I didn't know and one I had recently met. I had been contacted by Mr. and Mrs. Woods at the beginning of the year about providing couples counseling at their marriage retreat. Mrs. Woods had attended one of my seminars the year prior and felt my counseling approach would mix well with their Christian-focused style of relationship training. For the past ten months, I had been conversing back and forth with the Woods, planning for this event. In preparation, the Woods had forwarded to me marital questionnaires completed by each participating couple. I began skimming through the folders that I had created for each couple as the plane pulled away from the terminal and the flight attendants began to conduct the safety briefing.

"Andrea, did you pack my swim trunks?" Lem asked, completely ignoring the First Class flight attendant who was demonstrating how to put on an oxygen mask less than two feet away from him.

I shot him a disgusted facial expression. "No. I threw those nasty, holey things out at the end of the summer. You had those trunks when I met you eight years ago. How long were you expecting them to last?"

"Forever." He laughed.

"I could tell. They have plenty of shops on South Beach where we can get you a new pair."

He pointed at me as if a parent chastising a child. "Since *you* threw out my old pair, I'll let *you* handle getting the new ones." Then, laying his head against my shoulder like a toddler, he said, "I'm about to take a nap. Get me some orange juice and some of those good cookies when the lady comes by with the cart."

I shook my head at my immature, yet charming husband and turned my attention back to the files on my lap. In addition to creating a folder for each couple, I had labeled each with a potential problem area (PPA) based on the results of my evaluation of the questionnaire. I'd developed my own classification system that consisted of the most common nine complaints/issues couples typically presented in counseling: Money, Infidelity, Communication, Children, Sex/Intimacy, Career/Educational, Intrapersonal/Mental Health, Spiritual, and Other. Some couples' issues revolved around one PPA while others had multiple PPAs negatively impacting the marriage. By pre-categorizing each couple on the retreat, I could mentally prepare myself for working with them, although the reality was that in marriage therapy, anything was liable to happen and nothing could be assumed. I picked up the files, one by one, and read the index card I had attached to each of them.

Martin and Lydia Woods. Married twenty-three years. Couple has three adult children. Martin is an accountant. Lydia is a family educator. PPA: Children.

Franklin and Tamela Day. Married thirty-six years. Couple has five adult children. Current pastor and first lady of Well of Hope Christian Church. PPA: Spiritual, Other.

Carl and Kelly Bradford. Married eleven years. Couple has two daughters. Carl is a real estate agent. Kelly is a high school science teacher. PPA: Intrapersonal, Communication, Other.

Jordan and Sarah Larks. Married seventeen years. Couple has a pre-teen son. Jordan is a police officer for DeKalb County. Sarah is a call center customer service representative. PPA: Intrapersonal/Mental Health.

Eric and Amber Hayes. Married twenty-one months. Eric has a daughter while Amber has no biological children. Eric is the CEO of Hayes & Ross Realty. Amber is the owner of Sweet Tooth Oasis and Sunrise Sunset Childcare Center and co-owner of Hayes-Ross Realty. PPA: Sex/Intimacy, Communication, Children.

By the time I finished reviewing the files, we were high above the clouds, and the flight attendant was approaching our row with beverages and snacks. I slid the files into my laptop bag and sighed again. Although I hadn't met these couples yet, I could sense the tension from some of their questionnaires. Call it the Holy Spirit or even intuition, but something inside told me that it was going to be a very interesting week.

Amber

How could I love my husband so much and dislike him so strongly all at once? The emotions I felt seemed bipolar or schizophrenic or whatever the disorder that caused people to have more than one person living inside their head, controlling their every move. I knew I wasn't crazy, at least not yet. However, being married for the past twenty-one months was slowly driving me insane. It wasn't that I hated marriage or even my beau, Eric, but dealing with the same issues day in and day out could make the most mentally stable person certifiable.

Okay, I was over-exaggerating a little. We had one issue, one major issue that was causing a dozen other problems and in the process, making home life miserable for me—we couldn't have a baby. It wasn't that we hadn't tried or that I couldn't get pregnant—I had been pregnant at least three times—but every pregnancy ended in a miscarriage and I was frustrated out of my mind. To make matters worse, over the past few months, sex had become painful for me, causing me to no longer want to be intimate. Eric, being a typical man, always seemed to want physical affection, but I refused to let him touch me if it meant me being uncomfortable. I had been to the doctor about my problem, but I was told that medically, I was healthy. Nonetheless, the discomfort continued until about three months ago when I shut down the love factory. Until I got to the bottom of what was wrong with me, there would be no baby making, not that we were making babies anyway.

Of course, Eric didn't understand and complained frequently. I knew I was taking a big risk, and by withholding sex he might be tempted to cheat on me, but after last year's drama with him and Jacqueline Johnson, I triple-dog dared him to think he could get away with being unfaithful. For those of you who don't know our situation, when I married Eric, I owned three businesses and he worked for me as an office manager for my real estate company. My wedding gift to him was giving him majority ownership of the realty and making him the CEO. Some people have given me flack over this decision, but I did it because, one, there was no way that as my husband he could continue working underneath me and I didn't want him to have to start all over in his career, and two, he was a big reason why the company had become successful, so it only seemed right to trust it in his care. Well, he accepted the position of CEO and everything was fine until he took on a female client named Jacqueline who calls herself Jay and is the owner of an international chain of fitness centers. The moment that woman saw my husband, she decided it was her mission to end our marriage and make him her man. Not! Eric loves me and didn't want her, but that didn't stop him from lying to me about who she was. I thought Jay was a guy. When I found out that the Jay he was gallivanting around the city with was a woman who was trying to sink her claws into him, I almost hit the roof. But I'm saved so I didn't lose it . . . that much. To his credit, his intentions were admirable; he was only trying to sell a commercial property to a major client. After Jay's property closing, and because of some connections he made through her, the realty really blossomed and began to get quite a few high profile clients and commercial sales. But back to the point I was making, the entire episode severely affected our marriage, and I have to admit, I considered kicking him to the curb. After that mess, I dared him to think he could cheat and remain married to me. No, I wasn't the one.

It was almost a whole year later and I still didn't have a child. Well, not one of my own. In the middle of the Jay scandal, Eric was going to court for custody of his daughter, Jonelle. He actually won which was a surprise to all of us considering most cases do not swing in the father's favor, and his ex-girlfriend Lena put on an Oscar-winning performance, trying to lie her way to victory. The judge saw through her charade and awarded primary custody to Eric. Jonelle immediately began living with us and visiting her mother on the weekends, holidays, or when we'd go out of town, like in this case.

We were sitting at the gate in Atlanta's Hartsfield-Jackson International Airport waiting to board the plane, on our way to Miami for a marriage retreat. I looked over at Eric who was merrily chatting with his friend and employee Carl, who was also going on the retreat. I wanted to roll my eyes at both of them, but I reserved an indifferent demeanor because Lydia and Martin

Woods were sitting across from me and I knew Lydia always had her eyes on me. Not only that, but my church's pastor and his wife were sitting next to them. I would have to be on my best behavior on this trip being surrounded by all of these people who would definitely call me out if I wasn't acting Christ-like and virtuous. I looked around at the small group that were coming along with us. In addition to the people I already named, there was Carl's wife whom I had met at a few company outings, and a woman from my Wife 101 class, Sarah, and her husband, Jordan. Lydia had informed us that a psychologist would also be coming to the retreat to work with us, but I didn't see her at the airport, so I assumed she'd meet us there. I just hoped she knew what she was doing because I didn't know how much longer I could keep Eric at bay, and truthfully, although (at times) he made me feel exasperated, I deeply loved the man and didn't want to lose him.

Eric

"The captain and crew of flight 4070 with service from Atlanta, Georgia, would like to welcome its passengers to Miami, Florida. The local time is 1:12 p.m., and the weather in Miami is sunny and humid with a temperature of 88 degrees. Please remain seated with your seatbelts buckled until the plane comes to a complete stop and the seatbelt sign is turned off. Thank you for flying American Airlines, and we hope you enjoy your stay in Miami or wherever your final destination may be."

By the time we all exited the plane, made our way through the concourse to the baggage claim, retrieved our luggage, and loaded into a pre-arranged shuttle bus, it was close to 2:30 p.m.

We were staying on South Beach which was about a fifteen minute drive from the airport in light traffic. The shuttle bus driver was a foreigner—I believe he said he was from South America—who kept asking us questions about where we were from and telling us how much fun we were going to have in Miami. He said a few other things, but Amber and I were near the rear of the shuttle, and between the side conversations by the other group members and his thick, Spanish accent, I couldn't make out what he was saying.

Despite the shuttle having air conditioning, the hot sun beamed relentlessly through the glass window making the inside of the vehicle feel stuffy. I was relieved when we pulled up in front of the Beacon Hotel, our accommodations for the retreat. The hotel was retro, but apparent exterior and interior renovations fit in perfectly with the South Beach skyline. The Beacon sat directly across the street from the beach, nestled between another hotel and Johnny Rockets which is an old school style burger joint.

The hotel lobby was white, accented with orange décor. White walls, white chairs, orange lamps, orange pillows. This theme continued throughout the hotel, even into our guest room; all of the white and orange making me feel like I was trapped on a knock off version of the TV show *Miami Vice*. Nonetheless, the accommodations were extremely comfortable and the moment I laid down on the all-white, memory foam-cushioned, king sized bed, I knew I was in paradise.

This vacation was exactly what Amber and I needed to get our marriage back on the right track. I hated to admit it, but ever since I had messed up last year with the lies about working with Jacqueline Johnson and caused Amber to have the first miscarriage, my marriage had been broken. I thought, or maybe I was just hoping, that everything would return to normal after we agreed to work through our issues and spent our anniversary in the Dominican Republic. Yet, here we were, nine months after our vacation, now having another pseudo vacation and all was not well in the Hayes household. Our businesses were doing great, but careers and money had never been a major issue between us. I guess with so many couples arguing over finances, our lack of struggle in that area was a blessing. But every couple had their crosses to bear and one of ours was having a child of our own.

Honestly, Amber didn't come across as the kind of woman who desperately wanted to be a mother, but regardless of how she appeared on the outside, on the inside, it was tearing her apart. I knew that having my daughter, Jonelle, live with us was probably magnifying the issue. As a man who had a child previous to my marriage, I didn't have to wonder or worry about legacy. Yes, like most men, I would have loved to have a son to carry on my name, and because I cared about my wife, I wanted to give her the baby that she desired. Yet, if for some unknown reason we never procreated, I could live with it, but I knew that Amber could not.

The proof that she couldn't handle not becoming a birth mother was demonstrated in the fact that she had ceased from being intimate with me. After a total of three miscarriages in one year, she just stopped trying. Now, I understood her being frustrated and disappointed, but how could she have a baby (naturally and legitimately) if she wasn't willing to have sex with her husband? Truth be told, her behavior was frustrating and disappointing me. If her goal was to make me feel how she felt, she had successfully achieved it. More than just making babies, I wanted to touch my wife, hold her, comfort her, and be close to her, but she wouldn't allow any of it. I was desperately hoping that this trip, along with the marriage classes and counseling, would mend our brokenness. I really loved Amber, but how long could any young, able bodied man who was married to an attractive woman tolerate abstaining from sex? I didn't want to be unfaithful like my father, so I had been praying long and hard that God would not tempt me more than I could stand. Jesus be a fence around me and these bikini wearing women on the beach!

Lesson 2: A Time for War

A time to love, and a time to hate; a time of war, and a time of peace. (Ecclesiastes 3:8)

Dr. Wilson

Because Lem and I came in to Miami from New York, we got to our hotel later than the rest of the group. Once we checked in, I called Lydia and let her know that we had arrived. She asked me to meet her on the fourth floor so that she could show me where I would be holding my counseling sessions. My husband was feeling a bit jet lagged despite the natural excitement of being on South Beach, so he decided to take a nap while I met with Lydia. I changed out of my northern gear into a maxi dress, freshened up, and left my snoring husband in the room as I ventured out to meet Mrs. Woods.

The hotel only had one elevator which was terribly slow, so I opted to use the stairs to ascend from the third floor to the fourth. Lydia waited for me in front of a room at the end of the hallway, smiling sincerely as I approached.

"Dr. Wilson. Such a pleasure to see you again," she said as I neared her.

She reached out and gave me a big, motherly hug, which I returned obligingly. "Call me Andrea. It's great to see you too.

Thanks for inviting me," I said. "I'm so glad to get away from that crazy weather up North. It's absolutely beautiful here."

"I know. Makes you want to vow to never return home."

"Exactly."

"I cannot express how thrilled we are to have you here with us," she said while turning around and unlocking the door to the room. She opened the door and entered, holding it ajar so that I could enter as well. I glanced around the room which was slightly bigger than the one I was staying in. Instead of having a king sized bed, it contained a queen sized bed, a desk, a sofa, and a lounge chair.

"This is where you'll meet with the retreat participants for your therapy sessions," Lydia said. "This hotel is a bit older so it doesn't have meeting rooms, but I figured you could use the sofa area in this queen suite as a makeshift office. All of the couples are staying on the second floor and your room is on the third, so this suite should be far enough away from everyone else to preserve privacy. Will this work for you?"

"Oh yes. This will be fine," I said as I scanned the room again.

"You'll find that this hotel's walls are sound proof. I've stayed here before and although the party never ends outside, you won't be able to hear a peep of the noise once you come inside." Lydia began to walk out of the room and I followed. Once we were back out in the hallway, she passed me the small, electronic keycard to the room.

I stuffed the keycard into a side pocket in my purse. "That's good to know. So what's next on the agenda?"

Lydia leaned against the white wall next to the room's door. "We are going to meet on the beach at six o'clock. We have a tent set up there where we will hold our group meetings. In the information packet I sent you, there is a map that will direct you on how to get to the tent, but it is just across the street and down the beach a short distance, so you shouldn't have any trouble finding it. This meeting will be a short, introductory gathering, and then we'll all have dinner together directly afterwards at a nearby restaurant. We still have a couple of hours until six, so feel free to rest or check out the beach."

"Actually, I think I'm going to do a little shopping. My husband needs a new pair of swim trunks so I'll visit a few of these boutiques since we have some down time."

Lydia stood up straight. "That's sounds like a good idea. I need a new bathing suit myself. Mind if I join you?"

"No, not at all. The company would be nice."

A little over an hour later, Lydia and I had walked down Ocean Drive several blocks and stopped at a few of the shops along the way. There were more stores including popular name brand retailers on Washington and Collins, which were the streets that ran parallel to Ocean Drive, but we decided to wait until later in the week to explore them. We waded through the crowd, cutting through tourists and locals. Most were enjoying the diverse eateries with outside seating that ran along the sidewalk. As we snaked our way across the mob, Lydia spotted another boutique and we agreed to give it a try. This particular shop had a wide selection of men's and women's beach wear, and Lydia and I were able to find what we were looking for. The store had a "no returns" policy, so Lydia tried on the bathing suit she wanted while I went to the register to checkout. Buying for my husband was easy because I could look at a pair of shorts and know they would fit him. Plus, he liked to wear his clothing a bit loose, so I would always try to buy a size or two bigger than his actual fitted size. If I had to buy the item for myself, I would have been back in the fitting rooms with Lydia, trying it on. For some reason, women's clothing seemed to be hard to judge visually.

A Hispanic woman rang up my purchase and bagged up the swim trunks in a plastic bag. For payment, I handed her the debit card for the bank account that Lem and I shared. The woman swiped the card twice, then passed it back to me and said, "The card is declined."

"Really?" I asked surprised.

She nodded. "Yes. I tried twice. Do you have another card or cash?"

"Yeah, sure," I said, shaking my head in disbelief. I pulled out my debit card for my personal bank account and paid for the trunks. By the time I signed the credit card receipt, Lydia had come out of the dressing room and was headed toward the register. I watched her as she made small talk with the cashier, but my mind was a million miles away, trying to figure out why my joint bank account couldn't cover a $20 pair of swim trunks. It didn't make any sense. Lem and I mutually deposited a specified amount of money into this account each month to pay our house bills and cover additional family related expenses. Lem usually wrote out the checks for the bills, so I rarely monitored the account. Most times when I spent money, I would use money from my personal accounts, but when I did use the joint account, I would give Lem the receipt so that he could deduct the amount from the bank register. Considering the fact that I had just made a $1,000 deposit into the account a week prior, I couldn't understand why the bank would reject the meager $20 purchase.

I was so deep in thought that I didn't notice that Lydia had completed her transaction and was now standing in front of the shop's door, waiting for me. "Andrea? Dr. Wilson?" she called out to get my attention.

I blinked out of my trance. "Huh? Oh, sorry. I sort of spaced out."

"Are you okay?"

I began walking toward the exit. "I'm fine. Just thinking."

Lydia nodded then looked down at her watch. In recognition of the time, she said. "It's already 5:30. I guess we need to get back to the hotel, drop off this stuff, and get ready to meet the rest of the group."

I quietly followed her out of the shop, still pondering over my bank account situation. If I had my way, I would have immediately addressed the issue with Lem, but by the time we got back to the hotel, there was barely enough time to wake him up and get to the meeting site without being late. In addition, if the conversation didn't go well, I knew it would leave me in a sour mood. As the hired therapist in the group, I didn't want the group's first impression of me to be one that was tainted by a bad temper or tardiness, so I ignored my desire to get to the bottom of the money issue and proceeded directly to the scheduled retreat activity.

Amber

As much as Eric and I wanted to peruse South Beach, fatigue won out and caused us to catch a nap before the welcome meeting and dinner. We awoke around 5:00 p.m., took showers, and were dressed and out the door by quarter to six.

In order to get to the retreat tent, we had to cross Ocean Drive which was a high traffic street, walk through a small park area to get to the entrance of the beach, and then travel down the beach about 50 feet. Wearing sandals, walking through the warm sand was a bit of a chore, and I was relieved when we made it to the midsized green tent. The walls of the tent were rolled down and secured, only allowing us entrance through the large opening in the front. Inside, there were no chairs and the floor was the actual ground, forcing Eric and I to remain standing along with the other couples who had arrived before us. Within minutes, Lydia and Martin entered the tent, as well as a woman and man that I was unfamiliar with. I immediately assumed that the woman was the psychologist, Dr. Wilson, and the man was her spouse. Once the last couple from our group, Sarah and Jordan, walked in, Martin called the meeting to order.

"Welcome to Well of Hope Christian Church's marriage retreat. Most of you already know us, but for the few of you who don't, I am Martin Woods and this is my wife, Lydia Woods. We have been charged with overseeing this retreat and teaching a daily class that will hopefully strengthen your marriages. As a group, we will be here in sunny Miami, Florida for seven days. So, get ready to work and play in one of the most popular vacation destinations in the country."

Martin looked at us sympathetically and said, "We apologize for not having any seating in the tent for you. We can't afford to leave chairs in the tent when we are not here because beachgoers might take them. All of you have two beach chairs in your hotel room closest. We ask that starting tomorrow during the class sessions that you bring those chairs with you for seating. You don't have to worry about bringing them in the morning for prayer because we will just stand during that time.

"Before we do anything else, let us start off this week properly — with prayer." We all bowed our heads and closed our eyes as he began to pray. "Heavenly Father, we thank you for this time and this season to come together to build, strengthen, and celebrate marriage, especially in a world that seeks to undermine, devalue, and destroy the union of husband and wife. Thank you for allowing us to arrive at our destination safely, and we ask that You continue to provide us protection and traveling grace and mercy while we are here, and as we return to our individual homes. Now Father, we ask that you bless our time together and help us to use it wisely. Bring to the forefront any issues that are crippling our marriages, and give us the strength and courage to resolve these problems before we depart from this place. If there is any unforgiveness in our hearts, reveal it to us and help us to let go and let You heal our broken places, because we know that unforgiveness is the root to bitterness, resentment, dissatisfaction, and ultimately, failed marriages. Use the teachings that Lydia and I have prepared, as well as the counseling sessions with Dr. Wilson, as an instrument to break every yoke and stronghold that remain in our lives. We put our trust in You and not ourselves, and we believe that by the time we leave here, our marriages will be made whole. We ask these things in the mighty name of Jesus. Amen."

Amens filled the tent. Martin lifted his head, opened his eyes, and nodded at Lydia who then began to speak. "This brings us to a big question that I know you all are dying to ask us—why did we decide to host a marriage retreat on South Beach? Yes, this is very atypical, but there is a method to our madness. Usually, marriage retreats are held somewhere quiet and isolated to help the participants shut out the rest of the world and focus solely on their marriages, and quite possibly, to hear from God in the process. As much as that is an awesome experience, life isn't like a cabin in the woods. Life is like South Beach—busy, loud, tempting, and even chaotic at times. It's easy to focus on your marriage when you're in the middle of nowhere and your spouse is your only sidekick, but the real world is full of people and issues, constantly attempting to distract you from your priorities. That is why we chose South Beach, to simulate the chaos of life. If you are able to focus on your marriage, grow, learn, and hear from God in this environment, you're more likely to be able to maintain what you've gained when you return home."

Martin interjected. "I know it may seem as if we are throwing you all into the lion's den, and in a way, we are. Our goal for this retreat is to teach you all the art of war. The enemy has been waging war on our families for way too long and it is time that we started fighting back. When the military is training their recruits, they don't take them to the Hyatt hotel, pamper them, and then expect them to be ready for the battle. No. They take them out to the wilderness, to environments that look closer to what the battleground may look like, they stretch them beyond their comfort zone to produce warriors. Now, lucky for you all, you do have cozy hotel accommodations, but being in an environment that has nearly any temptation and distraction you might face can stretch you and prepare you for the battle for your marriages. We will be training you how to take a hit and keep on standing."

Lydia smiled and said, "Your training will be threefold. Every morning we will gather at 6:30 a.m. for thirty minutes of couples and group sunrise prayer. At 7:00, you will be permitted to go and have breakfast. We will regroup at 9:00 a.m. for the Couples 101 class. You will then have the remainder of the day to spend with your spouse; however, every day you will have a set time to meet with our marriage therapist, Dr. Andrea Wilson. This will be a one-hour session held at the hotel that will give you the opportunity to work short-term with a licensed professional." Lydia walked over to the unfamiliar woman and put her hand on the woman's shoulder, signaling that she indeed was the psychologist. "We are very grateful that Dr. Wilson has agreed to come and participate in our retreat and handle some of the issues that Martin and I are not trained to deal with. The exact time of your scheduled daily appointment with Dr. Wilson can be found in your registration packets."

Lydia turned to Martin who concluded the meeting. "We encourage you all to enjoy yourselves while you are here. There are many dining options, activities, and sights in the City of Miami, so when you are not with us, please take advantage of this vacation. If you all have any questions, concerns, or emergencies, you have our cell phone numbers in your packets so that you can reach us. Because this is your first night and the actual retreat starts tomorrow, we have planned to have dinner as a group at one of the nearby restaurants. Unless anyone has any questions, we can all head there now."

When no one spoke up, the Woods took it to mean we were all in agreement. Everyone filed out of the tent and followed Lydia and Martin to the T.G.I. Friday's located on the corner of Ocean Drive and 5th Street. Lydia explained that they had chosen Friday's because of our group's size, knowing that it would be easier to reserve a table around dinnertime to accommodate us all, being one of the few indoor restaurants on the main strip. Personally, I was so hungry that I didn't care where we ate. We had an entire week to patronize the various restaurants in the area, so as long as we were seated quickly, I was grateful.

Eric and I were the first to sit down at our reserved table. Of course, Carl took the empty seat on the other side of Eric, and his wife sat next to him. Once again, I caught myself considering shooting both of them a nasty glare. I had no problem with Eric and Carl being friends, but we were supposed to be here to work on our marriage. I didn't want those two spending too much time engrossed in each other, preventing Eric and I from having our much needed time alone.

After we placed our orders, Pastor Franklin led us in a group prayer over the food, then we spoke amongst ourselves until our entrees were served. Midway through our meal, Eric leaned over to me and said, "Carl and Kelly want to hang out a bit with us after dinner. Are you okay with that?"

No! I was not okay with it. We hadn't even been in Miami for twenty-four hours and already we were attached at the hip to Carl and Kelly. When Eric initially told me that he had suggested they attend the marriage retreat even though they weren't members of our church, I suspected that it might not have been the best idea. It wasn't that I didn't like Carl. In comparison to Eric's brother, Nelson, and a few of Eric's fraternity brothers, Carl was a saint. Nonetheless, I simply didn't want Carl to distract Eric from our reason for being on this trip.

Now, Kelly was a completely different story. I didn't know her too well, but from what I had learned about her on our brief run-ins, I didn't care much for her. Atlanta was a keeping-up-with-the-Joneses kind of city. Many people were all about the façade of looking rich even if their pockets were really filled with lint. Kelly was the kind of woman who had started off living a modest life, but had allowed herself to get sucked into consumerism and pretense. From my conversations with Eric, I had found out that although she didn't overspend like many folks, she was nearly killing herself working two jobs just so that she could buy Prada and Chanel. Not only that, but she dressed and behaved as if she were twenty-five, single, and childless, instead of pushing forty and married with two kids. I was cautious about hanging around women like her; I didn't need any of that fakeness rubbing off her, onto me.

Eric must have seen the hesitant look in my eyes because he then said, "We're just thinking about going down to Fat Tuesdays. They have a pool table and we just want to play a game or two. We only have to go for an hour or so. I promise you that we'll do something together, just you and I tomorrow night."

He gave me a pitiful baby-please look and I gave in. "Okay, but I'm going to hold you to your promise tomorrow." I exhaled, relieved my husband was finally understanding me without me always having to spell everything out to him. Eric was a wonderful man, yet he wasn't as attentive when it came to me as I was of him. I could merely look at him and know exactly what he was thinking, how he was feeling, and what he might do next. He, on the other hand, was still struggling with figuring me out which made it frustrating for the both of us. I found myself often having to take the time to explain myself over and over again. But hey, that was marriage, or at least the early years of marriage. Right?

୶

Eric

After dinner at T.G.I. Friday's, Amber, Carl, Kelly, and I walked down Ocean Drive a block or two past our hotel to Fat Tuesdays. Fat Tuesdays was somewhat like a sports bar in the sense that it had a pool table and TVs that were constantly tuned in to ESPN or whichever game was airing. But the real appeal of Fat Tuesdays was their specialized frozen daiquiris that tasted like Kool-Aid, but were far from it. Back in my college years, my fraternity brothers and I would down a few 190 Octanes and spend the next morning paying for it with a massive headache. Yes, I grew up in the church, but as most Christians, I had my fair share of worldly experiences from pre-marital sex and having a child out of wedlock, to partying like it was 1999. I no longer lived my life that way, but plenty of my friends still did. I guess Kelly still did too because the moment we walked into the building, she ordered a Spiked Lemonade Daiquiri. Carl glanced her way, then looked over at me and shook his head, but did and said nothing to discourage her. I couldn't help but to quickly divert my eyes to Amber because I knew the way she felt about Christians drinking. Amber wasn't completely against alcohol, but she didn't consume it and preferred that others not consume it as well—at least not around her. The realty was that we were in South Beach, a geographical location that was known for its nightlight, complete with endless alcohol and clubs that didn't close until sunrise.

Just as I figured, Amber was eyeballing Kelly as if she had just dropped ten points on the Amber Ross-Hayes Approval Scale. Considering the fact that Amber barely cared for the woman, a loss of ten points probably meant Kelly was now in the negative. I guess Amber's best friend, Tisha, didn't have to worry about losing her BFF position during this vacation.

To me, Kelly ordering a drink wasn't as big of a deal as Amber and Carl was making it. I rarely consumed alcohol. I'd had enough of it back in college, and even then, I really didn't like the taste. I hated to see people drunk and inebriated, but I also didn't attack everyone that I saw with a drink in their hands with a sobriety sermon. Wasn't the first miracle that Jesus performed turning water into wine at a wedding? The way I saw it, unless there was an issue with misusing or abusing alcohol, the Holy Spirit should be the one to convict the person about their drinking behavior, not people. But hey, that was my opinion, yet because I didn't want to have a debate with my wife about it, I frequently kept that particular opinion to myself.

While Kelly was waiting to be served, Amber walked over to one of the empty tables near a television and sat down. Carl and I claimed the pool table and began racking up the pool balls. Carl took the first shot, making the break, and sending the triangle-shaped clutter of pool balls flying in every direction. A striped ball went into a corner pocket, and Carl said, "Stripes," declaring the striped balls as his challenge.

Before he took his earned next shot, in a hush voice he said, "She always does that."

I quickly assumed that she referred to Kelly and that he was still harping on her drink order. "It's just one drink and you all are on vacation . . . in Miami. Lay off her a little," I said, attempting to smooth things over before it became a major problem between them.

Carl shook his head at me and took his next shot—this time missing his mark. Carl was a pretty good pool player, but at that moment, he was distracted. "It's not just the drink. Kelly wants to be this young, twenty-something woman again. She has everyone at her part-time job thinking that she's twenty-six. How is she twenty-six when she has two school-aged children?"

"Y'all could have started early. It happens," I said jokingly.

"Yeah, but that's not the case here. No offense to you, but we had both of our kids within the marriage."

"None taken."

"She didn't used to be like this. But it was like the minute the girls got old enough to go to school, she decided that it was time for her to get her groove back. Started dressing in short, tight clothing, hanging out late with a bunch of women ten and fifteen years younger than her, spending all this money on designer labels like she's married to Donald Trump. She knows that I don't even have it like that, so what does she do? She gets a second job to pay for her new lavish lifestyle. Now, I appreciate that she's not being a financial burden on me, but my daughters are watching her act like this. What kind of message does that send to them?"

"Sounds like you and Kelly need to be on this retreat just as much as Amber and I. Maybe you should address this issue during your sessions with Dr. Wilson."

"Man, I hate counseling, especially when it's with a female psychologist. You know she is just going to side with the women. Remember, I've been to therapy before with my wife. I know the deal. Somehow, someway, we're going to end up looking like the bad guys."

"If Dr. Wilson is as good of a therapist as the Woods claim she is, she should be able to remain unbiased. All I'm saying is that you paid your money to be here, so you may as well take advantage of the included counseling sessions."

"Yeah, you're right." Carl looked over at the bar. By this time, Kelly had been served her drink and was sucking up the frozen beverage through a clear straw while bouncing to an old school, upbeat Whitney Houston track that was playing loudly through the establishment's stereo system. "Would you look at her? Man, let me tell you right now. I've been married almost twelve years and there are still days that I wonder if I married the right woman or if I ever should have gotten married at all. I'm not saying this to scare you. I just want you to be aware that all it takes is one issue to destroy a marriage. It doesn't matter how long you've been married or how much you think you love the person, one critical problem can eat away at everything you've built."

I looked over at Amber who was staring blankly at the TV screen. She wasn't interested in sports, so I knew her thoughts were not on the soundless basketball game that appeared before her eyes. I wondered if she was thinking about us—if she was questioning if she'd married the right man. I shifted my attention back to the pool table, took my shot, and said, "Let's hurry up and finish this game before my wife starts trippin' too."

Lesson 3: Who's Your Enemy?

Put on the whole armour of God, that ye may be able to stand against the wiles of the devil. For we wrestle not against flesh and blood, but against principalities, against powers, against the rulers of the darkness of this world, against spiritual wickedness in high places. (Ephesians 6:11-12)

Eric

On Saturday, Amber and I woke up at 6:00 a.m., washed our faces, brushed our teeth, threw on shorts and t-shirts, and headed out to the beach to meet everyone at the tent for sunrise prayer. There was a two-hour gap between prayer and our couples' class, so we figured we'd eat breakfast and take our showers during that time. Originally, we'd planned to wake up at 5:00 a.m. to dress properly for sunrise prayer, but that idea was negated when we returned back to the room from Fat Tuesdays the night prior around 10:00 p.m., and admitted to ourselves that we were still exhausted from traveling.

We were the last couple to walk into the tent, making it there at 6:30 on the dot. The moment we walked in, Martin asked us to form a large circle and all join hands. I ended up wedged between Amber and Dr. Wilson's husband, Lem. For a split second, I wondered what kind of marriage Lem and Dr. Wilson had with her being a psychologist who specialized in marriage therapy. I figured it was perfect. I mean, it would only make sense for a nationally acclaimed marriage counselor to have a problem-free marriage.

Before I could dwell on the idea of being married to a perfect woman, Martin began to pray, causing me to bow my head and focus. After a five-minute, heartfelt prayer, Martin ended the prayer with an "Amen," and the rest of us repeated, "Amen." He then instructed us to break up into pairs with our spouses, go out onto the beach, find a private spot, and to pray together for each other, ourselves, and the marriage.

Amber and I walked down near the shoreline and planted ourselves close enough to the water to feel it wash over our feet each time the tide came ashore. Although the time was early and the sun was just beginning to rise in the horizon, the air was still humid and warm, making the cool water a welcomed sensation. Birds flew by and called back and forth to each other. Periodically, a small breeze from the water would flow through the palm trees behind us, creating a fluttering sound that added to the beach's ongoing natural symphony. As much as I had groaned about getting up forty minutes prior, I was now glad that I did. Sunrise prayer was the perfect way to start our day, and I thanked God during my prayer for the opportunity to experience a new dawn with my wife.

By 7:05 a.m., we were headed back to the hotel. The Beacon served restaurant style breakfast outside, in front of the hotel on their patio. We allowed the hostess to seat us at a table for two despite seeing some of the other couples from our group also preparing to eat. Friday had been filled with us being constantly with the group, so as promised, I intended to spend the majority of Saturday alone with Amber. I was impressed by the assortment of items on the menu we could choose from that were complimentary for us being guests at the hotel. I ordered eggs, toast, sausage, and potatoes, while Amber order a Belgium waffle and a side of bacon. It was too early to talk, and we were still at peace from our morning prayer, so we sat in silence, enjoying the scenery and our food.

We returned to our room around quarter to eight and began to shower and dress for the day. We made it back to the tent at five minutes to nine—carrying our beach chairs, Bibles, and being well groomed this time. Even 9:00 a.m. was still pretty early, and beachgoers were scarce, providing us a level of seclusion we couldn't pay for later on in the day—especially on a Saturday. We set up our chairs and made small talk with the others until a few minutes after nine, which was when Lydia stood before us and began to speak.

"Welcome to Day One of our marriage retreat. As we stated yesterday, our goal is for you all to learn the art of war, and this will occur through these classes, your therapy sessions, sunrise prayer, and the other experiences you'll have while you are here," she said.

"Over the next seven days, you will be in training with your mate, learning how to fight together against the enemy. The realty is this—whether or not you want to fight, you are being fought against. Many of you may remember being back in grade school and having a bully pick on you. Some of you might have been the bully, so you can't relate, but for the rest of us, we hated that bully because often that person wanted to start a fight when we simply wanted to be in peace. We were going to school or playing, minding our own business when out of nowhere comes this bully and his or her friends—bullies rarely come by themselves—causing trouble."

Lydia chucked. "And you see, bullies are strategic. They never come around when you're strong or have help with you. No, they come along when you're most vulnerable, when you're alone, when they think they can easily overpower you. Bullies don't attack you when you're looking for a fight; bullies attack when you want to be left alone. The same principle applies to your marriage. No, your husband or wife is not the bully waiting to fight you, but trust and believe, there is a bully who is out there, looking to pester you, looking to defeat you, and he will wait until you and your mate are most vulnerable . . . and that is when he will attack. It doesn't matter that you're tired and don't feel like fighting; it doesn't even matter if you're not prepared to fight. Actually, that is what your bully hopes—that you won't be ready, that he can catch you off guard. Preparing you for the battle is why we are here on this retreat. I know many of you thought that because we're in South Beach, this was just going to be a vacation. This is way more than a vacation; this is Battle Boot Camp." Lydia reached into a straw beach bag, pulled out a baseball cap designed in a green camouflage pattern, and slipped it on her head as if we had just enlisted in the army.

"It is debated that the divorce rate among Christians is between 30-45 percent. I'm not talking about nonbelievers; I'm talking about us—people of faith, people who believe in God's Word which discourages divorce. But it's believed that we're getting divorces nearly as much as people out in the world. Why?" I sensed the question was rhetorical, yet she still looked around the tent as if she expected someone to answer. When no one spoke, she continued.

"God hates divorce, but loves His people. The enemy, however, loves divorce and hates God's people. He loves divorce because it destroys the basic human unit—husband and wife. Remember, man's fall was a consequence of the devil deceiving Eve then Adam to eat of the Tree of Knowledge of Good and Evil which was forbidden. Since the creation of man, the enemy has been consistently at work to destroy the relationship between God and man. It would only make sense that he would aim his attacks not only at Christians, but at our marriages."

She reached back into her large beach bag and pulled out her Bible. "Before I get too far ahead of myself, let's look at the Word.

Over these seven days, we will be studying Ephesians 6:11-18. This is a popular passage in the Bible about putting on the armor of God. Let's turn our Bibles to Ephesians 6 and read verses 11 and 12. I realize that you all might have different versions of the Word, but Martin and I prefer to teach from the Amplified version, so I will read out loud what it says. 'Put on God's whole armor—the armor of a heavy-armed soldier which God supplies—that you may be able successfully to stand up against all the strategies and the deceits of the devil. For we are not wrestling with flesh and blood—contending only with physical opponents—but against the despotisms, against the powers, against the master spirits who are the world rulers of this present darkness, against the spirit forces of wickedness in the heavenly—supernatural—sphere.'

"Um," she moaned and nodded as if to express her agreement with the scripture. "I've already begun teaching you this, but let me make it clear just in case any of you haven't understood what I've been trying to say. Your spouse isn't your enemy. I know he or she gets on your nerves. I know he or she does silly things or is impossible to get along with. I know you sometimes wonder why you ever got married and some of you wish you could go back to being single again. I know some of you are married to someone foolish, who seems to wake up making mistakes. But no matter how frustrating, how annoying, how crazy, or how evil your spouse may seem, they are not your enemy. Your enemy is the devil and his angels. Don't be confused and do not be deceived. The majority of the stuff that your spouse says and does that angers you is a product of the devil's influence. You're pointing your finger of blame at the wrong one."

I was tempted to glance over at Carl to see if he heard what Lydia had just said. The one thing that I loved most about the way the Woods (and many other anointed Bible teachers) taught the Bible was how they seemed to always cover the exact topic we needed to hear at the exact moment we needed to hear it. I didn't look at Carl because I didn't want to be obvious, but I did try to peek at Amber using my peripheral sight. She was another one who needed to hear this message. There were plenty of times in our marriage when I would have bet money that she had pegged me as her enemy. Then again, the message was really for all of us. I had to admit, I had also done the same, especially when she cut me off from the lovemaking.

Lydia continued. "Let me say this—I know you all love to use the term hater to describe a person who tries to block you from a goal or bring negative energy to a situation. Well, the devil is the biggest hater of them all; he invented hating. You haven't seen a hater until you've seen the devil at work. All of these little people around here that you think are so awful and jealous of you, they aren't anything in comparison to your true enemy. He hates you because God has created you to reign with Him, and the devil has lost his place in glory. The devil wants to take you down with him because one, misery loves company, and two, he wants to hurt God by hurting you.

"Ephesians 6:12 tells us that we are not at war with flesh and blood; we're not at war with other humans. This fight is spiritual; this fight is against our true enemy, the devil and his crew. Remember when I was talking about bullies and how they rarely come alone? That's the enemy's tactic. The devil is limited in himself, he can only do so much alone, so he has gathered a whole army of fallen angels, evil spirits, powers and principalities of darkness to help him bully God's people. You might not want to fight them, but baby, they are picking on you and pushing you. They're knocking you upside the head and stealing your lunch money. You can either get beat up every day or you can decide to stand up and fight back. The key to dealing with bullies is not being afraid. Most bullies bother those who are scared to fight back. Once you show a bully that you can take him, most times he'll leave you alone, afraid you'll turn the tables and hurt him instead."

Lydia closed her Bible and said, "In order to be ready to fight a war, you have to know who your enemy is and who your enemy isn't. If you don't know who you are fighting against, you are likely to wound or kill your ally. That is what's happening in marriages every day. We are wounding our allies—our spouses—daily because we think that they are the enemy. We have absolutely no clue who is the real enemy so we are out there with a gun, shooting down everyone who comes within ten feet of us. If you don't get anything out of today's lesson, get this: your husband or wife is not your enemy. Recognize that this is a supernatural battle and that your true enemy isn't who and what you can physically see. It is who and what you can't see that is killing your marriage. Put on your spiritual lenses and see the truth about who and what you're fighting against."

I wasn't always the most vocal person about my thoughts and feelings, so I did something very typical of myself—in my mind. I said with passion and conviction, "Amen."

Lesson 4: A Time to Lose

A time to get, and a time to lose; a time to keep, and a time to cast away. (Ecclesiastes 3:6)

Look to yourselves, that we lose not those things which we have worked for, but that we receive a full reward. (II John 1:8)

Amber

The first couples' class had been stimulating, but I wasn't surprised. Eric and I pledged to come to this retreat because we had both experienced the amazing relationship ministry of Lydia and Martin Woods. Lydia had begun the course, laying the foundation, exposing the true enemy in our marriages. I actually never thought that Eric was my enemy, but honestly, there were many times when we seemed to fight against each other instead of for each other. Often, I felt as if we were in competition, but I had always felt that way with men. I guess I was still learning how to be that virtuous woman who was secure enough to let her man be the leader without fearing that he would end up leading our family astray. Was it that I didn't trust Eric or that I was just a control freak? Probably a bit of both. Maybe the real issue was that I was still figuring out how to trust God. Well, one thing I was certain of, I was looking forward to our counseling session with Dr. Wilson which followed directly after the couples' class ended.

We met with Dr. Wilson in a room on the fourth floor of our hotel. I was slightly surprised that our counseling sessions would be taking place in a hotel suite, but then again, we were on South Beach with the Woods. Nothing would be as expected.

We sat down on an orange sofa while Dr. Wilson pulled the separate lounge chair closer to us and sat in it. She was wearing a long, yellow, cotton dress with spaghetti straps and gold sandals. She had a head full of long, natural locks which she wore pulled away from her face, up in a ponytail. She looked young—I suspected she was around my age—mid thirties or so. The idea that she could have went to school with me threw me off. In my fantasies about this trip, the psychologist was at least in her fifties. Nothing against younger women because I was very successful for my age, but when it came to therapy, would someone who had lived just as much life as I be able to help not only us, but the other couples like my pastor and first lady who were well into their sixties? Only time would tell.

"Good morning. Eric and Amber Hayes?" she asked, looking down at a notepad that laid in her lap.

"Yes," Eric responded. "That's us. Good morning."

"Good morning," I chimed in.

"Great," she said. "Well, let me get all of my introductory items out of the way so that we can talk more about you guys. I'm going to tell you a little bit about myself, and then I am going to explain about the sessions."

Eric and I nodded, and she continued. "As you know, my name is Dr. Andrea Wilson. I am a licensed psychologist who works primarily with marriages and families. It is my goal and passion to help people find their way through the hard times together. I believe that it is often the storms of life that challenge the solidity of our relationships. I like to think that what I do is similar to a lifeboat in the midst of the ocean. These sessions won't save your marriage, but they will provide a safe place for you to meet and address your issues as you come into agreement, do the work, and wait for God to rescue you.

"I am married—you've met my husband, Lemuel. We've been together for eight years, married for five. I'm going to answer in advance the question that is on most couples' mind when they meet me so that we can get past it. Can someone who is as young as I am and who has only been married for five years help you? Well, the answer is up to you. This has absolutely nothing to do with my age or my marital status. This is about your marriage. If you are focusing on me, you're missing what needs to be dealt with in your own marriage. Like I said, I am not here to save you or your marriage; I am simply a vessel, providing an opportunity for you two to work through the hard stuff. The rest is up to you all and God. Understand?"

Eric and I nodded again. I felt as if she had read my mind and quickly put my doubts to rest. Lydia was right—she was good, and we hadn't even gotten to the counseling part yet.

"What we will do over the next several days is considered brief therapy," she said. "Normally, marriage counseling might take place over months, sometimes years. But because we only have seven days together, we won't dive into all of your issues— we don't have the time for that. Instead, we will focus on one or two priority problems you all are having, and attempt to work through them as much as possible, leaving you two with some potential, practical solutions that you can take home with you. Also, my counseling style is faith-based, so please feel free to discuss your relationship as it relates to your belief in God, and be aware that I will incorporate your belief system into my work with you. Any questions so far?"

I looked at Eric, and he at me. Both of our faces were blank, signaling to the other that we couldn't think of anything at the moment. We shook our heads to say no. I was starting to feel like a little kid in school with all of the head nods and shakes.

"Good. Let's start with you, Eric. I know that you already filled out the pre-retreat questionnaire, but I would like to hear this from your own mouth. Please give me a quick summary of what marriage is like for you and give me one issue that you would like to work on during our time."

"Uh," Eric started, looking at me with uncertainty as if he felt he needed my permission to be honest with her. I gave him a quick head nod, urging him to go on and tell her. I guess that was the signal that he was seeking, because he then said, "Mostly, I feel like my marriage is good. I love Amber and we're really blessed. She has helped me to become a better man, and I am very proud to say that she's my wife. We don't argue a lot, but I know she gets upset with me from time to time. For me, there's only one major glitch in our marriage . . . our sex life."

I had a feeling he would want to work on the whole sex thing. I was a little embarrassed that he'd brought it up so soon. I mean, we had just met the lady. I secretly wished he would have waited at least until the third session, you know? Give us a chance to make sure the woman is legit. I cast my eyes downward to the floor to hide my shame.

"Tell us about your perception of the problem with your sex life," I heard Dr. Wilson say.

"It's not just my perception—it's the truth. We're not having sex. We haven't had sex in months."

"Is there a particular reason? Obviously, you must want to be physically intimate since you're bringing it up in the session. Am I right?"

"Yeah. I definitely want to be able to touch my wife, but she . . . she pushes me away. I suppose it's because of all of the miscarriages."

I looked up at Eric. I couldn't believe he was telling this stranger all of our business—well all of *my* business. I knew we were here to deal with our problems, but now that we were sitting in the counseling session, talking to a real psychologist, I didn't want to discuss them anymore. I just wanted to walk out of the door and never come back. He looked back at me. He must have felt the intensity behind my glare because he turned his head away from me.

There was silence for maybe sixty to ninety seconds before Dr. Wilson spoke. "Amber, I know it may be difficult to hear what your husband is saying. Sex is a very personal topic and you have every right to decide if you want to discuss it or not with me. Your husband wants to talk about intimacy issues during our time, but these sessions will only work if you are willing to also talk about it. So tell me, are you willing?"

Was I willing? That was a good question. A huge part of me wanted to scream out no, but there was a small part of me that wanted to make my husband happy and to bridge the massive rift between us. If I didn't deal with my feelings here and now, would we ever grow beyond this blockage in our marriage?

I put on my big girl panties—meaning courage—and said, "Yes, it's uncomfortable to bring you into our bedroom—metaphorically speaking—but if it's what we need to resolve, I am willing to give it a try."

She offered an empathetic smile. "That's all any of us can ask for, your willingness to try. So tell me your perspective. What do you see as the underlying issue of why you two aren't having sex? Is Eric correct about the miscarriages?"

I shrugged. "I guess that's a part of it. Dr. Wilson, I love Eric, and it's not that I'm trying to be the prude wife that wants to deprive her husband of sex. It's not even an attraction issue." I could feel Eric's eyes back on me. I knew that I had just agreed to talk about this matter, but rapidly, I was regretting it. I had never been one who hold back my opinion or feelings, so why did I find it so difficult to admit the truth?

I focused my eyes on Dr. Wilson who sat there peacefully and patient, waiting for my confession. I let out a heavy sigh before saying, "I . . . I've just . . . lately it's just been painful. I tried, but for some reason after the last miscarriage, sex became painful for me. I can hardly get through it. That's when I stopped completely. I went to my doctor, and he said there's nothing wrong with me. But something has to be wrong. We've never had any problems in that area, and now, all of a sudden, it's like I can't. I just can't." I paused for a second because my emotions were getting the best of me. I opened my mouth to speak again, but the words came out sounding like a whisper. "I don't know what's wrong with me."

No, no, no! I was about to cry; however, I didn't trust Dr. Wilson enough to show her my emotional side. The tears were welling up, yet I blinked them back. I took a few deep breaths to calm myself. I could do this; I could be strong about this. I had spoken these words to my gynecologist, to Eric, and even to my best friend, Tisha, with no troubles. Now for some strange reason, I had said a few sentences to this psychologist woman and I was ready to fall apart. Seriously, Amber?

"Thank you for being honest, Amber. And please know that if at any time you feel this is too much to handle, it's okay to take a break or whatever you need to do to cope."

I nodded, but didn't dare to speak. I was on the edge, and I knew if I spoke one more word, the dam would break and I would lose the battle with my tear ducts.

Dr. Wilson looked at me. I felt as if she were looking through me. Her eyes were steady and determined, yet soft and caring. I waited for her to say something, but she didn't. She just looked at me as if she expected me to tell her more. Wasn't it Eric's turn to speak? Ask him another question! I wanted to tell her that she needed to leave me alone, but I couldn't open my mouth because my strength depended on me keeping quiet. I would not be the woman who cried during the first counseling session. I refused to.

Then the doggone woman beat me with an unanticipated move. She passed me a box of tissue that has been sitting on the end table nearest to her. I did not want to accept it, but it would have been rude to reject it. The moment I reached out for the box and took it into my hand, the tears began to fall. The box's weight seemed to triple and it became too heavy to hold. I couldn't believe that she had made me cry with one simple, intentional move. I hated her.

I jumped up from the sofa. The tears were falling quickly and I could feel a wail rising up my throat. Oh no! I would not let her see what she had done. She was not *that* good of a therapist. It was both of their faults—hers and Eric's—and I would not give either of them the benefit of allowing them to watch me break down. I dropped the tissue box onto the floor in front of me and raced out of the room. I could hear Eric calling my name as I yanked the door open, but there was no way I was turning back. I just needed to get back to the safety of my hotel room before that wail reached my tongue. I couldn't hold it back much longer. I passed the elevator and took the stairs, two at a time, running down to the second floor. I unlocked my room door not a moment too soon. The second I zipped inside, the wail consumed me and the best I could do to contain it was to fling my body onto the bed, stuff my face into the pillow, and let it out.

Eric

Amber ran out of the counseling session like a grizzly bear was chasing her. I called out to her and was even prepared to chase after her, but Dr. Wilson raised her hand, spreading her five fingers out to alert me to stop. I gazed up at the psychologist in confusion. Why wouldn't she want me to go comfort my wife who was obviously hurting? She gave me a firm look, her expression communicating for me to leave the situation alone. As much as I didn't understand her tactics, I conceded, figuring she knew how to handle these matters better than I did.

The echo of the door slamming seemed to vibrate through the room. I sat, allowing my back to rest against the fibers of the orange sofa, waiting for Dr. Wilson to decide what would happen next.

After a silent minute, she sighed and said, "You can't fix her."

"What?" I felt slightly offended by the statement.

"Amber, your wife. You can't fix her. I know you want to. Men like to fix things. You think if you go racing after her that you can make her feel better, but you can't. Amber is going to have to choose to be healed and only God can grant that wish for her."

I wasn't following Dr. Wilson. I mean, I understood the whole men wanting to fix things idea. Yes, I loved my wife and if there was something I could do to make her life better, I wanted to do it. And yes, I got the whole God healing her part. But I wasn't comprehending what I—Amber's husband—was supposed to do in the meantime. What if Amber never chose to heal? Would our marriage continue to lack passion and intimacy? That was simply not an option for me.

"Dr. Wilson, no disrespect, but what am I supposed to do? Sit here twiddling my thumbs? That's not the kind of man that I am. It's my job to support and protect my wife."

"Eric, I agree, and it appears that you are doing a good job. It's apparent that you truly love your wife and are wholeheartedly committed to her. I wish I could say the same about all of my clients. And I do want you to console your wife. But I also want you to consider two things first. One, I want you to give her a chance to feel the way she feels. If you are always trying to stop her tears, she won't fully experience the emotions that she needs to go through in order to move past them. Two, I don't want you to try to be her savior. She already has a Savior and His name is Jesus. It hurts to know that she is in pain because the two of you are now one flesh. When she hurts, you hurt. But just like she can't fill your void, you can't fill hers. God always reserves that job for Himself."

I nodded and exhaled. She was probably right. Unconsciously, I might have been trying to do God's job. I had never thought about it in that way. Maybe that was why my efforts weren't working.

"I'll try to hold back," I managed to say despite feeling overwhelmed by the conflicting emotions that I was feeling. I badly wanted to rush to my wife's side, yet I also didn't want to stand in God's way.

"Good. Let's talk for a few more minutes, and then I would encourage you to wait at least an hour before going to look for her. I can tell that Amber is a very strong woman, so she'll be fine. But give her enough room to breathe, okay?"

"Okay."

We talked for about twenty minutes more. I told her about how I used to work for Amber and all of the drama that led up to us going from employee-employer to husband-wife. I also told her about the three miscarriages that had occurred over the past year. Amber was no doubt fertile. It seemed as if every time I touched her, she ended up with a plus sign on the home pregnancy test. Nevertheless, the longest she had ever carried a child was six months before the pregnancy terminated itself. That was the first time. Since then, twice she had gotten to the two month point before her body rejected the fetus.

Dr. Wilson was a great listener and seemed genuinely interested in helping my marriage. Before I left her improvisational office, she suggested that we pray together about the situation. I held her hand as she took us before the throne of grace.

"Almighty God, thank you for bringing this couple to this retreat to work out the issues that threaten their peace and joy. Only You have the answers, only You know what will heal them and make them whole again. Losing a child is difficult, but You are able to give them back everything that was stolen from them. Comfort them, restore them, and be glorified through their testimony. In Jesus' name. Amen."

"Amen," I repeated.

I entered our hotel room two hours later. It was almost one o'clock and I wanted to check on Amber and see if she wanted to have lunch. I had spent the between time walking along the beach and airing out my thoughts.

Amber was sleeping like a baby, so I turned on the TV, making sure the volume was low enough not to disturb her, and watched an action flick until she awoke an hour later. Her eyes were puffy and red and her hair was tousled as if she had gotten into a fight—and lost.

"Hey, babe. You okay?" I asked.

She nodded.

"It's close to two. You hungry? Do you want to grab something to eat?"

She glanced over at the alarm clock to confirm the time. Slowly, she rolled out of the bed and lumbered into the bathroom. I heard the shower turn on a few seconds later. I refocused my attention back onto the movie until she was ready to re-enter society—which was thirty minutes later.

Lesson 5: A Time to Speak

A time to rend, and a time to sew; a time to keep silence, and a
time to speak. (Ecclesiastes 3:7)

Therefore, my beloved brethren, let every man be swift to hear,
slow to speak, slow to anger. (James 1:19)

Dr. Wilson

I'd had a long day. From 10:00 a.m. to noon, I had therapy
sessions—first with Eric and Amber, then with Carl and Kelly.
Both of those consultations had been emotionally draining, so I
appreciated my hour lunch from noon to one. Then from 1:00 p.m.
to 4:00 p.m., I met with Franklin and Tamela, Jordan and Sarah,
and Martin and Lydia, respectively.

At four, I closed down the makeshift office and headed out to
the beach. I needed some alone time before I met with Lem for
dinner. I still hadn't spoken with him about the bank account. I'd
intended to have the conversation with him after dinner the night
prior, but he had a serious case of sleepiness after eating a heavy
meal, so I just let him go to bed. After being with that man for
eight years, I knew it was futile to try to have a conversation with
him when he was half-asleep. I would just end up frustrated.
While he slept, I pulled up our joint bank account online to
investigate the matter myself. Our account was overdrawn nearly

$100. I saw my recent deposit, as well as previous deposits we both had made, yet there were checks that had been written out that had depleted the funds and they were not for household bills. I was mad enough to spit, and looked over at my irresponsible husband in anger. I didn't know who the checks were written out to, my bank only provided the check number and amount. A million wayward thoughts flew through my mind as to who was being paid with our money. A business debt? A get-rich-quick scheme? Another woman? A drug dealer? Okay, so my imagination was getting the best of me. I would have to confront him and get to the bottom of the missing funds. I avoided the conversation that morning when we'd awoke for prayer. I wanted my energy to be positive when I met with the couples for the first consultations. Nonetheless, without a doubt, I would be calling Lem out at dinner. I would not let the situation fester in the back of my mind anymore. I just needed to release my day and the weight of my clients' problems from me before I went in to deal with the issues within my own marriage.

I found a beautiful, large beach umbrella that had been left behind by some person or group. I claimed it temporarily as mine. Underneath it, I laid a thick, blue beach towel down on the warm sand and plopped down, starring out at the aqua water. One by one, I allowed each of the therapy sessions to play through my mind. It was a method that I had picked up over the years as a way to not carry client stress home with me. I found a serene place and mentally reviewed each case, writing down notes on any thoughts or feelings that captured me about the session so that I could let them go for the evening and return to them if necessary the next time I went back into work.

Eric and Amber Hayes. I should have known when the first session of my day was drama filled that it would set the tone for the remainder of the day. The wife was in a lot of emotional pain, much more than her husband recognized. I could tell that he didn't understand the deep level of disappointment and sorrow his wife was experiencing, although he wanted to. Amber was strong, too strong for her own good. Her need to be in control appeared to be preventing them from having a breakthrough. I knew plenty of women like her. When she ran out of the session, my suspicions were confirmed. She didn't leave because she didn't want my help, she left because she didn't want to appear weak. Too many women never received the restoration they needed in their lives because they were too busy saving face. If this couple was going to make progress during this week, it was going to take the wife pulling down her defenses and letting her husband, me, and even God in. Weakness was not the enemy — pride was.

Carl and Kelly Bradford. This couple was a classic case of what happens when one spouse has a midlife crisis. Kelly walked into our session wearing a bikini top and a wraparound skirt. From their original questionnaire, I knew she was forty. Yes, they were on vacation, but to present herself in counseling in that kind of clothing at her age screamed, "I don't want to get old!"

I purposely asked Kelly for her input and what she wanted to work on during counseling before I questioned Carl. "I just want my husband to act like my man and not my daddy. I mean, when did he get so boring? I hate the way he tries to keep me from enjoying my life. I keep trying to tell him, YOLO!"

"YOLO?"

"YOLO. You Only Live Once."

Carl interrupted. "You see what I'm dealing with?"

"What *you're* dealing with? What about what I have to deal with?" Kelly asked, noticeably offended.

"Let's bring it down a notch," I intervened. "Carl, what do you want to work on?"

"I just want my *adult* wife back, instead of having to raise three kids—my two daughters and this one over here."

Kelly rolled her eyes at him and popped the piece of gum that was in her mouth.

"Carl, you said you want your adult wife back. That implies that she hasn't always acted this way. When did she change?"

"It's been a while, but the biggest changes have occurred over the last six months or so. I know that this is more than likely just a phase, but I am really concerned about how her behavior is impacting our children."

"Our girls aren't thinking about me," Kelly said before popping her gum again.

"Is that the truth or what you want to believe?" I challenged her.

"It's the truth," she responded with a hint of an attitude.

I let it go. My goal wasn't to judge her or make her feel that I was on her husband's side, but in all actuality, her husband was right. She was acting like a fifth grader. Then again, I could understand why. They had been married for almost twelve years which based on their age meant they had gotten married in their late twenties and probably dated several years prior to that. Although it was common for couples to start a family in their twenties, some people who took this road felt as if they missed out on a part of their youth. Those years when all of their friends were still hanging out and having a good time, they might have had to reel in those desires for the sake of taking care of home life. At some point, they might start feeling old, like life is slipping away and that they only have one chance to revive their fading existence. Enter the midlife crisis. They convince themselves that they should be someone else or have something that represents youth, even if the changes they are making threatens to uproot their entire lives. Only an honest look in the mirror or a come-to-Jesus moment could cure them of their reckless behavior.

The rest of the session with them continued in tense arguing between the two. From time to time, I intervened and contained the bickering from escalating out of control, but for the most part, I allowed them to speak their peace. They obviously needed a safe place to get their feelings off their chests. Once I felt they had sufficiently expressed themselves and began to merely repeat their complaints, I would redirect the conversation, but it probably would take a session or two of fighting to get there.

Franklin and Tamela Day. The Days were a sweet couple who sort of reminded me a lot of my grandparents—when they were still alive. The Days were in their sixties and were clearly still in love. Franklin was everything you would expect in a good pastor—compassionate, friendly, a little humorous, steadfast, and sincere. Tamela was a tad feisty, but knew when to lay down the law and when to hush. After one session with them, I wanted them to adopt me, but I was sure my parents wouldn't like the idea very much.

When asked what they wanted to work on during counseling, Tamela said, "Franklin is a great man of God and I believe that there is still work for him in the Kingdom, but I can tell that he gets down and sad at times. A lot of our friends and family members are dying off as we get older. There was a time when death seemed far away, but now, it seems to meet us at every turn. Plus with Frank being the pastor, he performs many of the eulogies for deceased members. I think it becomes too much for him sometimes."

I shifted my eyes to him. "Pastor Day?"

"Please call me Franklin." He sighed. "My wife is right. She knows me well. I'm not afraid of death because I know that to be absent of the body is to be present with the Lord. I guess I just feel like I spent so many years learning how to live, and now I have to spend the rest of my years learning how to die."

End of life issues. They were always a difficult topic for me to counsel people about. Death was inevitable, and counseling someone about anything related to death was straight depressing. Usually bereavement counseling included helping people to build their relationship with God so that they could feel peaceful about their eternal destination. But with the Days being committed Christians who were certain of their salvation, how would I comfort them or redirect their thoughts on God? They were probably more familiar with the Man upstairs than I was. I would have to pray for guidance on how to work with them. I typically prayed for all of my clients, but I would need a triple dose of wisdom to be of assistance to the Days. One thing about me, I never overestimated my ability to work with a client. There were people that I was unable to help. I feared Franklin and Tamela might be two of those people.

Jordan and Sarah Larks. Can you say post-traumatic stress disorder? Jordan was a prime candidate for psychotropic medication. I knew that before we parted ways at the end of the retreat that I would need to recommend a psychiatrist in Atlanta to him and suggest he get evaluated for anxiety medication. He appeared before me as very tense and somewhat apprehensive as if he didn't trust his environment. I tried to make him feel comfortable and relaxed, but his distress showed on his face 24/7.

When I asked them what they wanted to work on, Sarah confirmed my suspicions. "I would like to see my husband get help for his anger and nerves. I'm actually surprised he even agreed to come on this trip because I usually can't get him to go anywhere new with me. He doesn't like to be in places that he's not familiar with. He says it's unsafe. He likes routine and this is definitely outside of the routine."

"What about you Jordan? What would you like to talk about during counseling?" I asked him.

"I don't know. I guess what Sarah said," he responded.

"I see you're a police officer. That's a very dangerous job. I'm sure you've seen a lot of crazy things that the rest of us couldn't imagine," I said.

"Yeah. You have no idea." He looked relieved by my validation of his position.

"He was also in the military for eight years, the Marines," Sarah added. "He did two tours in Iraq."

"I see. Well, let's start there. Tell me a little about your experience in the military," I said to Jordan.

"Being in Iraq was no walk in the park, especially for the Marines," Jordan said.

The rest of the session was used to discuss Jordan's time in the military. He didn't want to talk about certain aspects of combat which was expected. Very few veterans told everything. I observed how his body tensed up when he spoke about memories that made him uncomfortable or upset. He shut down a few times during the session. He would definitely need more psychotherapy than I could offer, and I didn't want to open too wide of a door to his problem since I knew my services were limited. I decided that I would use the remainder of my time with them discussing how his anger and anxiety negatively impacted the relationship, and provide them with tools handling day to day stressors rather than trying to resolve his psychological issues.

Martin and Lydia Woods. The Woods were my favorite couple already. I know it's probably not politically correct for a psychologist to say she has a favorite couple, but hey, it was the truth. It wasn't that this couple didn't have problems—every couple had their crosses to bear. However, the Woods had mastered the ability to fight for the marriage and not against it. They were respectful towards each other, even when they didn't agree. They'd learned not to take everything personally, and they were great at perceiving each other's needs. They truly operated on one accord, as one flesh, which was the desired state of all marriages. Lem and I hadn't even achieved their level of oneness and I was a marriage therapist.

Even their individual answer to my question of what they wanted to work on during our counseling session was the same. It was evident that they had discussed and agreed upon what they wanted to accomplish in advance.

"We would like to work through our feelings of loss and emptiness connected to all of our children being adults and out of the house," Martin said.

"I believe it's called Empty Nest Disorder or something like that. We looked it up online," Lydia said.

"Very close," I said. "Empty Nest Syndrome. Well, if you all looked it up, you should have a good idea of the symptoms. How long have your children been out of the house?"

"Babygirl just left for college in August. She was the last to leave. The other two are a sophomore and a senior," Martin said.

"It was difficult when our son and oldest daughter left, but we always still had the baby. But now that she's gone . . . it feels like there's this big hole in our lives," Lydia said.

"I understand. What are the names of your children?" I asked.

"Martin Jr. is the oldest, then there's Alexis in the middle, and Nicole is the baby," Lydia smiled and said proudly.

I leaned in towards them. "Listen, from now on I would like you to refer to your children by their names, especially the youngest, Nicole. You may not be aware of it, but the both of you call her some form of the word baby. As long as you continue to view her as a baby, you won't be able to let her go. She's an adult and should be referred to as one. I know she will always be your baby, but if you want to fully accept this transition in your lives, you will have to also embrace her as a woman."

They agreed to work on the name issue, and the rest of the session we spent discussing what it was like to watch each of their children grow up. I figured if I let them air out some of their good and bad memories of their children on day one, then on day two we could move on to their experience with watching each child leave the home. Working with the Woods would be a pleasure and a much needed emotional break from the draining sessions that were certain to result from a few of the other couples at the retreat.

By the time I finished jotting down a few notes about the Woods, I felt lighter and ready to deal with my own marriage. Emerging from the beach, I met Lem in the hotel lobby, and we walked down the strip a bit, deciding on a restaurant that served mostly seafood. We were seated at a table on the sidewalk, and our food and drink orders were taken rather quickly.

I didn't want to blindside Lem with accusations about our bank account, so first, I asked him about his day and told him about mine. I didn't divulge the details of the counseling sessions with him—that would have been unethical—but I did disclose to him that I was concerned about a few of the couples.

After several minutes of small talk, I said, "Honey, when I went to purchase those trunks for you, I tried to use our joint account to pay for them, but my card was declined. Our account is overdrawn. Do you know anything about it?"

"It's overdrawn?" he asked as if surprised.

"Yes. Almost one hundred dollars."

He let out a heavy sigh. "Dog," he said, but I could tell that he really wanted to curse. He rested his elbow on the table, closed his eyes, and laid his head in the arch between his index finger and thumb.

I waited for a minute. I wanted to see if he would offer any explanations on his own. The waitress brought over our drinks—

him a Sprite and me a glass of red wine. We thanked the server and began sipping our beverages.

When he didn't naturally clarify the matter, I said, "So what happened . . . with the bank account?"

He took another sip of his pop and scratched his head with his free hand. "I was hoping to get some money from this job I did not too long ago. I guess it still hasn't come in."

I nodded my head. I knew the way my husband conducted business. Sometimes he would do work for others and not get paid up front. Once the job was finished, the debt would be resolved. I didn't believe that was the right way to handle business. There were way too many what ifs like what if they didn't pay. We had spoken about him avoiding these kinds of contracts, but Lem was hard-headed, so he would have to get knocked upside the head a few times before the truth sunk in. I was okay with him getting beat up for his mistakes, but not when his punishment affected our livelihood.

"Alright," I said, coolly. "I guess I'm trying to understand how we got into the negative. There were several checks written out for amounts that were not our normal bills. Who were you paying?"

"I needed to pay the guys who worked for me."

What? Oh no he didn't. Any normal woman would have went off at that moment, but I was a trained professional. I knew how to talk to my husband like he was a man and not a child. *Be easy,* I reminded myself. "Why didn't you use your company bank account for that? Honey, that's a payroll issue, not something that should be coming out of our personal account."

He sighed again. I was waiting for his response when the food arrived. My tilapia appeared succulent and his steak looked even better, but I couldn't sink my teeth into the food until I got an answer. I guess he didn't agree because he began cutting his well-done slab of beef.

I bowed my head and said a quick prayer for both of our meals then picked up my fork. By the time I looked back up, he was inserting the first piece of meat into his mouth. I asked him again. "Lem, why did you pay workers out of our personal account?"

He finished chewing the sliver in his mouth and began to slice off another piece. "Because I didn't have the funds in my business account and I needed to pay them."

I put down my fork. "And you didn't think it would be wise to discuss this with me first?" I asked, my voice still even.

"Andrea, I knew you wouldn't like it. Plus, I needed to make a quick decision."

"Lem, how do you know what I would have liked or not liked? You didn't give me a chance to have any opinion at all. So what about our bills? Have they all been paid? What about the mortgage? Isn't it due any day now?"

He placed a forkful of mashed potatoes into his mouth. "About that . . ."

I frowned at him. "About what?"

"Do you think you could cover it this month until this money comes in?"

Crack. My levelheaded demeanor shattered. "Lem! I just deposited money into that account which you used to pay other people. Not only that, but three weeks or so ago, I put three grand in that account so that we could finish paying off my car. Where is that money? Are you telling me that you gave *all* of our household money to other people instead of paying our bills?"

"Sweetheart," he said. "This company owes me twenty thousand dollars. They should be paying any day now. When they do, I'm going to replace the money for the mortgage, pay off your car, and we'll be back on track."

I huffed. I was now agitated, so much so that I could not eat. My succulent tilapia was getting cold. "Lem, let me get this straight. You want me to pay the mortgage although I already gave you money toward the mortgage?" I looked around at the other South Beach patrons enjoying their evening. Too bad I couldn't say the same. I tried to compose myself, and asked, "How much can you pay towards it?"

"Nothing. I'm broke," he said nonchalantly, continuing to eat like he just informed me of the time or the weather.

"Excuse me?"

"I have maybe a hundred or so bucks in my personal account. I'm tapped out. I had to use all of my money plus some of ours to pay the guys. They were depending on getting paid. They have families to feed."

I couldn't believe him. How could he be so stupid? Psychologist or no psychologist, my husband was an idiot and I wished I could say so, but that would have been considered fighting dirty. Instead, I said, "You mean *all* of our money. And I was depending on you to pay *our* bills for *our* family."

I must have wounded his ego because he looked at me sternly. "Andrea, it's not like you don't have the money. Why are you acting like this?"

"What?"

Lem put down his fork and took another sip of his drink. "I know you have the money. This trip was free. That church paid for everything including giving you extra money for our meals. I'm sure you have at least a few thousand sitting in your savings account collecting dust, making money for the bank, and that doesn't include whatever is in your checking account which you never allow to drop below five hundred dollars. I'm not asking for a lot. I just need you to support me like I'm supporting you by coming on this trip. Please pay the mortgage this time so that we can keep our house and I promise that this won't happen again." He went back to consuming his steak.

Okay, now I was furious. "First of all, don't count my money. You have no idea how much money I have in my personal accounts. Secondly, we agreed to only spend money from our joint account on household related items. You broke our agreement. Now you expect me to bail you out?"

"I expect you to bail *us* out. This is *our* mortgage for *our* house."

"Oh, but it wasn't *our* decision when you spent *our* money, huh?"

Lem wasn't the arguing type, it was one of the things I loved and respected most about him. He had a way of making everything simple and plain, of just stating his position and being done with it. To me, it showed leadership and an ability to take control. Yet at that moment, I came to despise that quality when he said, "Sweetheart, we can argue about this all evening, but it's not going to change anything. I need you to help me out this time. Can you pay the mortgage?"

I shrugged to show him that I could play the indifferent role too. "Maybe I should just let them foreclose on the house. You're a home builder. You can just have the guys who are enjoying our household's money help you build another house for us."

He stopped eating and scowled at me. "Andrea, that's not funny. You're being selfish."

"I'm being selfish? Lem, you misused our money without my consent, put our livelihood in jeopardy so that you could save your business and I'm the one that's being selfish?" I yanked at my purse and pulled a fifty dollar bill out of a side compartment, slamming the money down on the table. "You know what? I can't do this with you right now. I'm going back to the room. Please have the waitress box this food up for me."

I stood up and started to walk away. Changing my mind, I turned around on my heels and came back to the table, towering above my still seated husband. "On second thought, don't wait up for me. I need some space. I'll sleep in my counseling suite tonight."

I rushed away from the restaurant, refusing to look back at my husband. By the time I walked the few blocks back to the hotel, my hunger started to re-introduce itself. I stopped at Johnny Rockets and ordered a burger, fries, and a shake. I stood and waited for the food, hoping it would come before Lem made his way back up the street. I didn't want to see him for the rest of the evening; Lord knows what evil words might have come out of my mouth if I did.

The food was handed to me fairly quickly and I jetted into the hotel, riding the elevator up to the third floor first to grab my nightgown, my toiletries, and a change of clothes for the morning. I made up an excuse in my mind during the short trip. If I was asked why I had stayed overnight in the suite, I would simply say that I wanted to focus on my client cases, and therefore thought it would be best to not be distracted by my own husband. To a certain extent, it was the truth. My quarrel with Lem had the potential to negatively influence my ability to remain unbiased and professional with my clients. I couldn't afford to be an emotional wreck during my sessions the next day.

I fled to the safety of the suite on the fourth floor with everything I needed to get me through the night. After munching down on the food, I showered, dressed for bed, and slid underneath the white comforter and sheets. Lydia had been right; Ocean Drive was in party prime with music blaring from every restaurant and club, but inside The Beacon, it was so quiet that I could hear all of my thoughts—even the ones I didn't want to hear.

Had I been wrong about the way I confronted Lem? Was I being unreasonable about not wanting to fix his mistakes? Yes, our house was in danger if the mortgage didn't get paid. Fortunately, the monthly payment was very inexpensive because Lem had built the house himself, yet we still had to borrow from the bank to pay for the materials, labor, and the land to build on.

We had agreed when we got into the loan to pay twice the amount due every month to clear up the debt in half of the time. We were only in a 15-year loan, so if we kept up with the double payments, we would be debt-free in about two and a half years. We were so close to finishing what we'd started; how could he do this to us now?

I stared up at the ceiling. I couldn't seem to stop my mind from ruminating on our financial situation. Did I have the money to bail us out? Yes, but that didn't mean that I wanted to use it in that way. I had saved up several thousand from doing speaking engagements, but almost half of that money I had deposited into our joint bank account so that Lem could pay off my auto loan. I figured since we only owed $3,000 more, paying it off would relieve us of that burden and free up money for other things we wanted . . . like children. Lem was one of those men that didn't want to have kids until he was "financially stable," if there were such a thing. I had been busting my butt to save up money and reduce our debt so that we could have a cushion and consider reproduction, because I certainly wasn't getting any younger. If I had to pay the mortgage and then turn around and pay my car note off, my savings would be depleted. There was no telling when this so-called money would come through, if it ever did. He still had a few people who had never paid him like they were supposed to, and once, we had to wait thirteen months for payment from a job of his. I just wanted to curse at the thought of one of his employees walking around spending my hard earned car payment money!

Maybe I was overreacting. I took a few deep breaths and tried to think about what I would tell a client who came into counseling with the same issue. *Kick him to the curb, girl!* No, I wouldn't say that. I might think it, but professionally it would be wrong. I would probably verbally slap the man's hand for making a bad decision without the woman's consent, and then ask the woman if she would rather be right or married. That advice sounded so good when I said it, but was a lot harder to live by. I knew that more than likely, I would have to bite the bullet and pay for Lem's foolishness, but I didn't like it, and I wouldn't make it easy on him. I pulled to covers over my head and prayed to God for peace so that I could get some sleep. That peace didn't come until three hours later.

Lesson 6: Go Hard or Go Home

Wherefore take unto you the whole armour of God, that ye may
be able to withstand in the evil day, and having done all, to
stand. (Ephesians 6:13)

Amber

The remainder of Saturday was peaceful. It seemed as if Eric
and I had an unspoken agreement not to discuss the
counseling session, or sex for that matter. We ate lunch at Wet
Willie's which was similar to Fat Tuesdays, but mimicked an All-
American style restaurant. After lunch, we headed over to
Bayside, a shopping area several minutes away from South Beach.
They had a bunch of outdoor and indoor merchants, so we took
advantage of the opportunity to load up on souvenirs, especially
for Jonelle, Eric's daughter. I could tell that Eric missed his child
immensely which stung a bit. That was the downside of marrying
someone who had children outside the marriage. There were
times when I felt as if Jonelle meant more to him than I did—and
honestly, who could compete with a child? Maybe his daughter
was one of the reasons that I wanted us to have a baby together,
so that I wouldn't feel like he had to choose between the two of
us.

After shopping, we stayed at Bayside a little longer and had
dinner at the Hard Rock Café. A live blues band performed,

providing entertainment along with the meal. By the time we returned to our hotel it was close to 9:00 p.m. I saw Dr. Wilson's husband climbing the outside steps in front of us, appearing somewhat distracted. I wondered where she was and why she wasn't hanging with him for the evening. I imagined that it had to be tough to juggle participating in the retreat, counseling us, and spending time with her hubby. I figured they probably were used to her having to work during these kinds of vacations and had somehow managed to make the best of it.

I even spotted Jordan and Sarah sitting out in front of the hotel, listening to Spanish music and watching a professional Latin dancer do the Bachata—a dance originating from Dominican Republic. I remembered the dance and music from my anniversary vacation to the D.R. earlier in the year. I would have loved to dance with Eric, but he rarely danced, especially not to Latin music. I figured Sarah was thinking the same thing about her husband because she was bopping and shaking in her seat, while Jordan kept scanning the area as if he was expecting someone to jump in front of their table and yell, "Boo!" I laughed at his obvious paranoia and proceeded to enter the hotel lobby with Eric.

On Sunday, we awoke less tired than the day before. Eric and I were able to get showered and dressed *before* going to sunrise prayer this time. Once again, we participated in a group prayer, then went our separate way in twos to pray as husband and wife. As I held Eric's hands, I silently prayed that God would help us to fix this sex and baby problem that existed between us. Eric and I were good together and we made a wonderful team, but there was just no way that I could be intimate with him if it was going to be painful. I found myself dreading the idea of him touching me, tensing up at the thought alone. Sex was about being relaxed and I simply could not do so. I prayed that God would heal me, whatever was wrong with my body, and make me able to carry a baby to full term. I knew that if I could just have one baby, everything would be okay. But in order to have a baby, I had to have sex—and I just couldn't bring myself to it.

Following prayer, we went back to the hotel for breakfast. This time, we invited Carl and Kelly to join us. I could tell that they hadn't had a good evening—fatigue and stress clung to their faces like caked-up makeup. Eric must not have gotten the nonverbal memo because towards the end of breakfast he asked them, "So what did you two do yesterday?"

"What do *we* do? Besides argue?" Carl's voice dripped with sarcasm.

Kelly rolled her eyes. "I blame it on that psychologist, Dr. Williams."

"Wilson," Carl corrected her.

"What?"

Carl sighed. "Her last name is Wilson. You would have known that if you'd been paying attention rather than trying to get your party on."

Kelly sucked her teeth. "Whatever. I know you didn't think that I was going to come all the way down to South Beach and not go to the club."

Carl shook his head in judgment. "I personally think they should have a maximum age limit at the club. If you're old enough to have a child that can also get into the club, you should be banned. Who really wants to see mothers and daughters partying together? A forty-year-old woman has no business dancing to music made by little boys that don't know how to pull up their pants and put on a belt, or little girls that think it's cute to rap and sing about how they want sex with no strings attached."

Kelly sipped on her Mimosa before saying. "Like I said yesterday in therapy, when did you get so old?"

"The same time you were getting old. You're just too silly to realize that you're old too."

"Whatever, Carl."

"Whatever," he mocked. "That's all you know how to say. Whatever." Carl looked over at Eric and I whose faces probably looked as awkward as the position they had put us in. "So how did your counseling session go?"

I coughed. Eric wiped his mouth and said, "It was okay. Look, we're going to get going, but we'll catch up with you guys at the couples' class."

I was relieved that Eric had handled the question vaguely. The last thing I wanted was Tweedle Dee and Tweedle Dum all up in our business. Eric and I left them and hung out in the hotel room watching TV until it was time for class. This time, Lydia sat in the crowd with the rest of us and Martin taught the lesson.

"Yesterday, my wife spoke to you all about knowing who your enemy is and isn't. I hope you all have taken some time to consider the lesson and begin shifting your perspectives about the nature of the battle. Today is Day Two of Battle Boot Camp. Now that we understand who we are fighting against, it's time to get ready for the war."

Martin opened his Bible causing many of us to do the same. "Turn with me to Ephesians 6:13. The Amplified version reads, 'Therefore put on God's complete armor, that you may be able to resist and stand your ground on the evil day—of danger—and, having done all—the crisis demands—to stand—firmly in your place.' Put on God's complete armor.

"If we back up to verse 11, it also tells us to put on the whole armor right before it tells us who we're fighting against. Once we are clear that this is a spiritual battle and our enemies are evil forces, we are then told again to put on the complete armor of God. Obviously, if it is said twice, this instruction is being emphasized for a reason. Usually when people repeat themselves it is either because they didn't think they were heard the first time or they want the other party to understand the importance of the direction. In this case, because the Book of Ephesians is a letter from Paul to the saints in Ephesus, more than likely Paul wasn't worried about not being heard, all of his words are clearly written in the letter. Therefore, it can be assumed that he wrote the words 'put on the whole or complete armor of God' twice because it was an essential directive that he wanted to make sure the people followed."

Martin continued to hold his Bible up in front of him, alternating between peering down at the scriptures and looking back up at us. "Notice that both times that he gave this instruction, he said right after it, 'that you may be able to stand.' Paul was concerned that when the enemy came, if the people were not prepared, they would not be able to survive the attacks against them. Today, God is saying the same thing to us. In every aspect of our lives, including our marriages, God is repeating Himself, reminding us to put on His holy armor, the battle gear that will allow us to survive even the strongest attacks of the enemy."

Martin finally closed the Bible and tucked it underneath his right arm. "Okay, let me give you an example. American football is considered somewhat of a dangerous sport. People can easily get hurt while playing the game. The goal of football is to get the ball across the field and score a touchdown. The team that scores the most points, wins. If you are the person with the ball, you need to be a little worried because everyone on the other team is out to tackle you and prevent you from scoring. Not only could they prevent you from reaching your goal, they could also physically injure you in the process of tackling you. But there's good news. One, you have teammates who have agreed to try to protect you from those who want to tackle you. Your teammates' job is to tackle them first before they get to you. However, often, the other team is too quick and are able to get past your teammates, and get close to you. The reality is that most times, you will get tackled and they will prevent you from reaching your goal. It's okay if they tackle you from time to time because your team gets many chances to try again to reach the goal. The biggest problem with getting tackled is that you don't want to get hurt. So here's the second piece of good news—you have equipment or gear to protect you. Professional football players wear knee pads, chest and shoulder pads, neck pads, thigh pads, hip pads, wrist pads, elbow and forearm pads, rib and kidney pads, helmet, mouthpiece, even an athletic cup to protect a man's most sensitive organ. A player would be foolish to go into battle against an opposing team without wearing proper protective gear. So why do we as Christians, get up every day and go into battle against our enemy without the necessary protective gear, especially considering that our enemy is far worse than someone wanting to simply tackle us over a football?"

I glanced at Eric who was eating the lesson up. I knew that the minute Martin started talking about football, Eric would be interested. Martin was a lot like Lydia in his teaching style, they both used a lot of relatable examples to make complex verses and ideas easy to understand. Even though Martin was going on and on about football equipment, I could feel what he was saying. He wanted us to see the significance of protecting our marriages by being spiritually prepared. Eric was nodding his head, so I knew he was also following along. I smiled about it and tuned back in to Martin.

"If we expect to be able to survive and not get hurt, if we plan on being able to stand up to the enemy and fight for our families, we must be prepared. We must come dressed and ready. We must do everything we can to arm ourselves for the battle. You know the saying, 'Go hard or go home?' Right now, God is telling us, be ready to fight, put on the whole armor or don't show up because you're going to get hurt. Showing up unprepared is not an option. Go hard or go home!"

Martin was right, and it hit me smack dab in my spirit. I would have to show up to counseling, ready to fight for my marriage or there was no point of me even being at the retreat. I said I wanted my marriage to work, but my actions demonstrated a lack of dedication. If I truly wanted healing, I needed to go hard, meaning that I needed to step up to the plate and not allow my fears to block my blessings. I had to take courage because getting back what had been stolen would not be an easy task, at least not for me. I took a deep breath in. Ready or not, the couples' class was ending and our therapy session was next on the agenda.

Lesson 7: A Time to Refrain from Embracing

A time to cast away stones, and a time to gather stones together;
a time to embrace, and a time to refrain from embracing.
(Ecclesiastes 3:5)

Can a man embrace fire and his clothes not be burned?
(Proverbs 6:27)

Eric

Amber and I had not muttered a word about the previous day's counseling session, so I wasn't sure if she intended to go back to therapy with me. I was a little surprised when she checked her hair in our hotel room's mirror after dropping off the beach chairs, then stepped back out into the hallway with me as if she also planned to head to Dr. Wilson's office.

"You're going?" I asked with uncertainty.

She offered a small smile. "Yeah."

"Oh, I didn't know if . . ."

She shrugged. "It's what we're her for, right?"

"Right."

In less than five minutes, we were sitting on the sofa in the counseling suite, across from Dr. Wilson, again. Her eyes appeared slightly red as if she hadn't gotten much sleep the night before. I couldn't help but feel a twinge of jealousy. She and her husband were probably up half of the night making good use of their cozy, king-sized bed, while my wife and I slept so far apart that I had to text message her that morning to see if she was awake. The thought of us wasting our vacation by not using the time we had away from Jonelle to do some baby making began to cause my blood to boil. This was ridiculous! I bit my bottom lip to refrain from yelling out my anger.

"I'm glad you're both back," Dr. Wilson said. She directed her attention to Amber. "After you left yesterday, your husband and I talked about how the two of you met and the interesting story that led up to your marriage. As you can imagine, I work with a lot of couples, so when I say this, please know that I am being sincere. Your husband really loves you. I think you know that already, but I am telling you this so that you can remember that this room is a safe place. It contains three people who really want the best for you—Eric, myself, and you. Do you understand what I'm saying?"

Amber nodded. "Yes. I'm sorry for leaving yesterday. It was just harder to talk about it all than I thought it would be."

"Amber, I get you. You actually remind me a lot of myself," Dr. Wilson said. "You're strong and ambitious, and sometimes us strong and ambitious people get in our own way. We don't like not being able to control our emotions. But don't think of counseling as a place that makes you weak. Think of counseling as a place where you can finally lay down all of that heavy weight you've been carrying. All of the times you had to be strong when inside you felt powerless, and all of the times you had to be perfect when you were really flawed—you can let go of all of that here and just be you. No pretense, no superwoman, no Mrs. Perfect, just Amber."

Amber's eyes began to water. I got nervous. I was still angry about the whole sex thing, but at the same time, I could see that my wife was enduring a lot of emotional turmoil. Amber didn't cry too often, so I took her tears as a sign that she was really struggling.

"Okay," Amber said.

Dr. Wilson continued. "Yesterday, you started to tell us about how sex has been painful for you. I want to explore that further, but before we do, let's talk about the miscarriages. I know that they are probably sore points for you and not easy to think about, much less talk about. Usually, I would build up to this, but since we only have six more days of counseling, including today, I would like to try to help you two as much as possible in this short amount of time. Do you think you can tell me about the miscarriages, Amber?"

Amber nodded and sniffled. Dr. Wilson passed me the box of tissues this time, and I sat them down on the sofa between Amber and me so that she could have easy access to them.

Amber cleared her throat. "I've had three pregnancies and all three have terminated themselves prematurely. Uh, the first time, I had gotten to the sixth month. We were so happy about the pregnancy. We even had a room in our house that was designated as the nursery. Early on in the pregnancy, my doctor told me that I had high blood pressure and that the pregnancy was risky. I'm somewhat of a workaholic, so he practically begged me to stop working. And for the most part, I did. I stayed at home and tried to do a few meetings and phone calls from my home office. It was killing me to not be allowed to run around Atlanta and manage my businesses. But . . . you know, doctor's orders. And then, one day I was in the office and I knew that my baby wasn't going to make it. I had started cramping that morning, and I tried to ignore it. I prayed and asked God to keep my baby safe. But even when I was praying, I knew. I knew it was over." Amber pulled one of the tissues out of the box and brushed it across both of her cheeks, catching the falling tears before they reached her chin.

"It was my fault," I blurted out, unable to take the guilt. I couldn't let my wife or Dr. Wilson continue to think that Amber was to blame.

Amber shook her head in disagreement. "It wasn't your fault, Eric."

"Yes it was. I stressed you out with the whole Jay and Lena thing. Your doctor said you couldn't have a lot of stress in your life and I was being selfish and . . ." I couldn't finish my sentence, but Amber knew what I was going to say. I was being selfish and stressed her out so much that it had cost us the life of our unborn child.

"What Jay and Lena thing?" Dr. Wilson asked.

Amber looked away, apparently still bitter about Jay. I looked away from Amber and my eyes met Dr. Wilson's. "Yesterday, I told you that when Amber and I got married, she made me the CEO of the realty. As much as I appreciated the gesture, it also felt like a handout. I didn't just want the position because we were married, I wanted to know I deserved it. I felt like I needed to prove myself, so I started pushing commercial sales. I had a wealthy female client named Jacqueline, but she referred to herself as Jay. She started to come on to me, and I thought I could handle the situation for the sake of getting her business."

Dr. Wilson continued to make eye contact with me. "Did you cheat?"

"No, I didn't cheat. But I lied to Amber and I omitted the truth about Jay being a woman when I knew Amber assumed she was a man. I went to this important party with all of the who's who people in Georgia, and I kept it from Amber, knowing if she knew I was going to the event with another woman who was trying to tempt me, that she would stop me from attending."

"So how did she find out? Did you tell her the truth?"

I glanced over at Amber who was still looking away. I hated to talk about her as if she weren't in the room, and even more, I hated to rehash this wretched story in front of her. "Yes, but only after I was forced to. My daughter's mom, Lena, and I were in court over custody of our child. Lena found out about Jay and used it against me in court. She was trying to make it seem as if I was having an affair to win her case. That was when I had to fess up to Amber. Right after that whole ugly situation, Amber had the miscarriage. So you see, it's my fault."

Dr. Wilson sigh and glanced in Amber's direction. "Amber, Eric believes that it is his fault. Do you blame him in any way?"

Amber stared down at the floor. "No. It just wasn't meant to be. If he's to blame then so am I. I wasn't supposed to be working at all, but I was. I was working the day of the miscarriage, even if it was from home. So, no. I don't think it's his fault."

"Alright. Tell me about the other two miscarriages."

Amber looked up at her. "Well, we went to the Dominican Republic in February for our anniversary. I guess we were having a really good time because I got pregnant again during the trip. I didn't even realize that I was pregnant until about six weeks. I immediately stopped working that time. I went on bed rest and everything. But it didn't help. Three weeks later, I lost the baby."

Amber dabbed the corners of her eyes with the tissue before continuing. "By then I was determined. I knew I could get pregnant, I just had to figure out how to keep it. So we started having sex all of the time so that I could get pregnant again. By mid-May, I was pregnant again. But this time it only lasted about eight weeks. Honestly, Dr. Wilson, I don't understand why God keeps taking my babies. Maybe I'm not supposed to have children, I don't know. It's not anyone's fault though."

"Why do you think that God wouldn't want you to have children?"

She shrugged. "I really don't know. Possibly because He's already blessed me with so much. Maybe there's a limit. You know the whole you can't have everything idea. From what people tell me, my life is close to perfect. I have career success, a good husband, money. Maybe that's as good as it's gonna get."

"Eric, what do you think?" Dr. Wilson asked.

"I've never thought about it like that. I don't see God as having those kinds of limits. Sometimes I wonder if this whole thing is my punishment for having a child out of wedlock."

Dr. Wilson blinked twice. "Do you really believe that God would keep Amber from conceiving because you sinned a long time ago?"

I wrung my hands together. "The Bible does say something about the sins of the father falling on the children or something like that. I'm not a Bible scholar, but I do know that there's a consequence for sin."

Dr. Wilson sat back in her chair. "I see. Let me review what I've heard from you all today. I heard Amber say that she doesn't blame Eric for the miscarriage, but she possibly thinks that she's run out of favor with God. And I've heard Eric say that he believes that he is at fault for the miscarriages, either because of the stress he has put on his wife or the sins he committed before marriage. Did I hear you both correctly?"

"You sure have a way of saying things," Amber said. "But, I guess that's the truth."

I nodded. "Yeah, in a nutshell."

Dr. Wilson clapped her hands together one time. "Okay, this has been a good session. One more topic that I want to quickly address before you all leave. Yesterday, Eric, you said that you two have not had sex in three months. Is that right."

"That's right," I said.

"And Amber, you stated that the reason for this is because sex has become painful, right?"

"That's right," Amber said.

"So over these three months, have you all touched or demonstrated physical affection in any other way such as kissing, hugging, or cuddling?"

"Not really." I probably spoke too quickly, but the words just seemed to spill out.

"We still kiss," Amber said as if she was trying to not make it look as bad as it really was.

I almost laughed at her comment. "Amber, a peck on the cheek or quick smooch on the lips is not really a kiss. My mother kisses me with more affection than you do."

Amber looked at me and narrowed her eyes. "I bet she does, momma's boy."

"I thought we resolved that issue," I said, slightly ticked off by her name calling.

"I thought we did too, but if you're going to compare me to your mother, maybe it's not as resolved as we thought," she responded, her attitude matching mine.

Dr. Wilson intervened. "Whoa, I think we just entered a completely different issue. Let's deal with one thing at a time. Amber, why aren't you being affectionate with Eric outside of sex? If painful sex is the issue, hugging or kissing shouldn't be hard to do."

Amber crumpled the sheet of tissue into the palm of her hand. I guess she felt she no longer needed it. "I don't get too close because I know that one thing will lead to another and then he'll want to have sex. It's easier to just not touch at all. He's just going to have to learn to control himself."

I grunted at her rationale. "That doesn't make any sense. So you're just gonna deprive me of all physical touch because you don't want to have sex? And how are you supposed to have a baby if we don't have sex? Immaculate Conception? Sorry to tell you Amber, but you're not the Virgin Mary and I'm for sure not Joseph."

Dr. Wilson put up both of her hands in the universal stop gesture. "Eric, Amber, let's bring it down a notch. We've made a lot of progress today and both of you should feel proud of yourselves for showing up and doing the work. Everything is not going to work itself out overnight, so just keep coming back every day. Honestly, it might get worse before it gets better, but if you really love each other and want this marriage, you won't give up.

"Eric, I know you're frustrated about not being able to touch your wife, but she is going through a lot of pain right now and you're going to have to be patient with her as God heals her. I would discourage you from trying to touch her until she is ready. Amber, Eric is not a mind reader. The only way he is going to know that you want to be touched or are ready to try again is if you tell him. I would like to see the two of you at least try to be affectionate during this trip. You don't have to have sex per se, but at least spend one night cuddling. It doesn't have to be tonight, but if and when you are ready, Amber, tell or show your husband. Okay?"

Amber

We ended counseling with prayer. I was glad that Dr. Wilson was a Christian counselor because Eric and I definitely needed a lot of prayer. I couldn't believe that he had compared me with his mother. I don't even consider my parents when I'm dealing with him. It was bad enough that I felt like I was in competition at times with his daughter for his love. I really thought we had gotten beyond the momma's boy problem. Since the beginning of the year, he had been doing well, putting his mother in her proper place—at her home with his father. I had been relieved to finally have my husband married to me vs. married to me and his mother. After all of this progress, here he comes comparing my kisses to his mother's. Seriously, Eric?

Okay, maybe it was just a minor setback, an innocent statement brought on by habit. I would give him a pass on that one, but he'd better never bring up his mother again while we were discussing intimacy between us or he really could forget about touching me for a long, long time.

The second therapy session had gone pretty well. I had dropped a few tears, but at least I didn't cry like a baby—the way I had done the day before. Dr. Wilson wasn't so bad. She knew her stuff—how to ask the right questions at the right moment. I was glad that she had told Eric to step off me and stop trying to touch me. I wasn't trying to be mean, but the more he pushed for physical affection, the more he made me not want to give it to him.

After we left counseling, we walked down the street and had lunch at a restaurant in front of another hotel. I was feeling a little tired, so we agreed to go back to the room after lunch, and I slept while Eric watched TV. A couple of hours later, I got up and we headed over to the beach. I read a book for a little while until Eric talked me into getting into the water with him. Of course, he couldn't be trusted and ended up dunking my head into the water, getting my hair wet. It was on! We proceeded into an all-out water fight, and when Lydia and Martin came into the water and joined in, the fight escalated into a battle of the sexes water war. By the time we finished playing an hour later, the watery battle grounds had recruited seven more couples who were strangers turned allies.

I could barely drag myself out of the ocean. I was exhausted from all of the screaming, splashing, and swimming. My stomach hurt so much from laughing that I didn't want to hear anything funny for days. Lydia and I dried off and took a seat on our beach towels as the guys changed gears and switched from a water fight into water football.

"That was fun," I said to Lydia as we watched the men run in slow motion in the water.

"Yeah, it was. Thank God it was in the water. If that would have been on land, I would have passed out after ten minutes," Lydia confessed. "It's amazing how water can hold us up."

I took in a deep breath. "I know. Makes me want to sign up for water aerobics."

She nodded. "So, are you enjoying the retreat so far?"

I smiled. "It's nice. I love the hotel, the food is awesome, and South Beach is amazing."

"What about the classes and the counseling?"

"Of course I *heart* the classes. You and Martin never let me down when it comes to Bible study. Even the sunrise prayer is helpful. I wasn't sure about having to get up so early, but it really helps set the tone for the day. Counseling . . . it's been hard. I like the psychologist, she's good. But you know, it can be emotional and painful. It's not easy."

"It wasn't meant to be easy. It sounds as if you're right where you need to be," Lydia said.

"You think so?"

Lydia chuckled. "If you told me that counseling was terrific and you were having a blast, I would have written a note to myself to never use Dr. Wilson again. It's not supposed to be fun. If you had a splinter stuck in your finger underneath the skin, getting it out would require digging into your skin to get to it. It would be more painful to take it out rather than leave it in. But then again, the discomfort of having a foreign object lodged into your skin would probably cause you to endure the pain of taking it out. Same thing with counseling. You have an uncomfortable problem, dealing with it hurts, but afterwards being healed is so much better than spending the rest of your life suffering."

She was right, but then again, she was always right. "See, that's what I'm saying. You always know how to make everything make sense."

"I think one day someone will say the same about you."

I laughed. "I doubt it."

"I don't. You're very smart, Amber, and I see God using you more than you imagine. You've already helped so many people through your businesses and at the church. And Eric is also developing so much into the man he's supposed to be. I know that you have a lot to do with his growth."

I looked up at Eric in the distance. "I sure hope so."

Lesson 8: A Time to Rend

A time to rend, and a time to sew; a time to keep silence, and a time to speak. (Ecclesiastes 3:7)

You who tear (rend) yourself in your anger, shall the earth be forsaken for you, or the rock be removed out of its place? (Job 18:4)

Dr. Wilson

Day two of the retreat was another brutal day for me. Doing conferences and retreats were a lot of work, actually more work than me seeing clients from my office back in Rochester. My favorite kind of work was when I did a singular speaking engagement like a seminar or a workshop. It was a limited amount of time—usually no more than two hours—I was paid, and I could be on my way. I enjoyed helping others, but counseling and working with people long-term was extremely exhausting. Several times over the past year I had considered quitting counseling and becoming a full-time author. Instead of giving so much of my emotional energy to individual clients, I could help many more people by putting out a few books. It would also give me more time to be at home with my husband and future children. Being an author would require a lot of travel as well, but I would have a bit more control over my schedule and wouldn't have to be gone as long. As my schedule currently stood, I was hired to do about a dozen of these marriage retreats a year which usually ran anywhere from three to seven days. If I wanted to one day be a parent, I would have to figure out a way to slow down on the frequent flyer miles.

In addition, if I didn't resolve my own marital issues quickly, I might not have to worry about being away from a husband or children—my husband might decide he was better off without me. The first time I saw Lem after the night prior's squabble was at sunrise prayer. I was a little surprised that he even showed up because Lem could be difficult when he wanted to be. If he hadn't showed up, I would have explained away his absence by saying he had slept in. Because I was working, he wasn't expected to come out to all of the activities. It was entirely up to him what he wanted to participate in and what he wanted to forgo. I assumed he came out to sunrise prayer to see me. He didn't like us being at odds, and the fact that I hadn't slept next to him more than likely made him need to see me to make sure that I was okay. Lem wasn't a bad guy in the least bit. He was actually a wonderful man who wanted to make me happy. But happiness was a temporary state based on circumstances that could not always be controlled. And at that moment, I wasn't happy.

Being one-on-one with Lem during couples' prayer was awkward. I could tell that he wanted to smooth the situation over with me, but it was 6:45 in the morning and I really didn't feel like talking about anything that would make me any more upset. I had only gotten a few hours of sleep and I was grumpy. I guess he noticed because he didn't attempt to provoke a conversation about our problem. Instead, we held hands and prayed for each other—in silence.

We agreed to have breakfast together after prayer ended, but that was also spent in silence. After being with Lem for eight years, quiet time didn't bother me. There were plenty of times when we would be around each other for many hours and not say a word. But this was different. Our muteness wasn't about enjoying not speaking, but all of the harsh words that would tumble out if we did.

Before we parted ways—to our now separate hotel rooms—he stopped me in the hotel's lobby by placing his right hand on the center of my back. "Andrea, are we going to talk about our financial problem, or are we going to smile and pretend for the sake of the group like everything is okay?"

As a licensed psychologist, I should have been more mature, but at that moment, I let my hostile emotions get the best of me. "I vote for smile and pretend. You?" I plastered on a fake Colgate smile to bring home my point.

He shook his head as if disappointed with me. Keeping his voice low, he said, "And you're the one that is supposed to be here helping these people stay married."

Low blow. Yes, I was being difficult, but I still couldn't get over the fact that he had spent our bill money on his employees without getting my permission. That was rule #1 in the marriage handbook—thou shalt not make major decisions without consulting with your spouse. For the last five years, we had adhered strictly to this rule and it had saved us from fallout moments like the one we were having. It seemed so unfair that he could make such a big, poor choice and that I should have to pay for it. And yes, I also knew that marriage was not about what was fair or unfair, but that didn't make me feel any better. I felt like I was sitting in the back of a classroom, taking the final exam, and equipped with a cheat sheet complete with all of the correct answers, yet I still wanted to go out on my own and see what would happen if I circled A instead of C. It was irrational, but it felt so good to be reckless.

"Yes, I am the one here to help these couples, and in case you haven't noticed, I'm good at what I do," I said while placing my left hand on my hip. "These people are depending on me to steer them in the right direction, and I don't need drama from you right now interfering with my ability to do my job. Especially since it seems as if I am the only one getting paid at this moment."

Okay, ladies, listen up. Never, ever, ever, ever, ever say anything crazy like that to a man. Let me say this a different way—never throw a man's money or lack thereof in his face. I don't care if you are Bill Gates rich and the sole breadwinner in your home, calling a man out about money is a guaranteed way to put your marriage on the fast track to divorce. Why? Simple. It's the mother-load of disrespect. Men were created to be the providers, so when you insult your man about money, you are basically telling him that he's not a man to the point that you've had to take over his position. It's a male ego thing. Reject Nike's motto and "Just *don't* do it."

I knew better. I had never in our three years of dating or our five years of marriage stooped so low, but then again, he also had never put us in such a horrible situation. This was exactly why I didn't want to be around him or talk to him because I knew that I was ripe to mutter some ice cold words. Honestly, this kind of behavior was not the norm for me when it came to my husband. Trust me, I had the boldness to cut someone down quickly, but I valued my marriage and my man too much to treat him that way. But one flash of Jimmy (who was one of his employees) spending my car payment money on lotto tickets (Jimmy was known for his addiction to the New York State lottery) caused me to verbally sucker punch my husband so hard that if we had been in a boxing ring, I knew he would be down for the count.

He glared at me in outrage and surprise. He didn't see it coming, he couldn't have. Truth be told, I barely saw it coming. I lifted my chin in insolence as if to say, "Yeah, I said it. What are you going to do about it?" Then the look in his eyes changed . . . to one of pain. I had hurt his feelings.

He stepped back from me and started to walk away. He got maybe four or five feet from me, then turned back around and said, "Who are you? When you figure out what you've done with my wife Andrea, the one who would never disrespect me like that, you know where to find me." With that, he disappeared up the stairs.

I attended the couples' class, but Lem was a no show. I figured he wouldn't come, and actually, I was glad that he hadn't. We would not have been able to stand next to each other and the rest of the group would have been aware that there was trouble in paradise. I had spent the hour between breakfast and the class praying, asking God to forgive me for being so cruel. By the time I finished pleading my case to the Lord, my spirit was humbled enough to go online and pay the mortgage. I still hadn't decided what I was going to do about my car note, but I figured that handling the mortgage was at least one step in the right direction. I felt lighter when I left the hotel for the class which was positive. There was no way that I could have carried that heavy load into my counseling sessions and still have been effective.

The couples' class was refreshing and uplifting, helping me to shed more of my foul attitude. Thank God for fast working prayers because His peace filled me and kept me thorough my five therapy sessions. Afterwards, I sat on the beach under the abandoned umbrella as I had done the day before, self-debriefing my cases.

Eric and Amber. I was very pleased at the progress made with Eric and Amber. After Amber's abrupt departure during Saturday's session, I wasn't sure how willing she would be to return to counseling and actually make herself vulnerable to the process. She shocked me by not only showing up, but pushing through the pain to speaking candidly about her miscarriages. I could sense that Eric was getting antsier about having to refrain from physical affection. They were starting to show signs of resentment—him due to her withholding sex, and her because he couldn't understand why. My guess was that her pain issues were psychologically oriented. The trauma from the miscarriages or even some hidden guilt and blame was more than likely the source of her problem. It was actually pretty common for women who had suffered a tragedy or abuse connected to their sex organs to internalize the hurt, leading to a sexually related disorder. The tough part would be getting Amber to trust Eric and I enough to disclose to us what was really going on with her.

Carl and Kelly. Kelly entered the second session wearing a tube top and shorts that had to belong to her daughters. Instead of looking like she was coming to couples' counseling, she looked as if she was interviewing for a job at Hooters. My first thought was that she was a fool, but my second thought was, who was I to judge? I had just emasculated my husband that very morning. Every wife, even marriage counselors, played the fool sometimes.

Once again, the session was filled with bickering. At least Lem and I weren't the only couple who had a bad evening. From what I had gathered, Kelly went out to a club on South Beach despite Carl's disapproval, and came back to the hotel at 4:00 a.m., smelling of liquor and some man's cologne. Of course, this didn't sit well with Carl who forced her to get up two and a half hours later and go to sunrise prayer still wearing her party clothes.

"At least you could have let me change," Kelly complained.

"Why? What are you trying to hide from the rest of the group? You're grown, remember? You can do what you wanna do," Carl mocked.

"You're just insecure. You're scared that someone else is going to steal me away."

"And you're delusional. What man, besides me, is really going to want a forty-year-old, married woman with two girls, who hasn't figured out that she's closer to getting Social Security benefits and the seniors' menu at Denny's than she is to winning

Homecoming Queen? You. Are. Old. Say it with me. Kelly. Is. Old."

Kelly sulked. "You're a hater."

"Yes, I am. I hate what you have on," Carl said and laughed.

I wanted to laugh with him, but it would have been unprofessional so I held back. I let them continue to trash talk each other until a few minutes before the session ended. It was actually quite entertaining. Carl could have been a comedian because he knew how to hit Kelly with clever yet hilarious lines at just the right moment. I figured it was one of the qualities that had attracted her to him in the first place. Carl wasn't "old" like Kelly was making him out to be. He had a very youthful spirit to him. He just wasn't trying to recapture something he felt that he'd left behind. He wasn't trying to prove himself to anyone; he was just accepting his position in life. Kelly, on the other hand, was grasping for the girl she used to be. Instead of embracing her development over the years, she was regressing in hopes that she could really turn back time.

Finally, I said, "Are you two done?"

"Huh?" Kelly asked.

"You've spent the first two sessions insulting each other. I've allowed it because I wanted to see what was really being communicated between the two of you. Even arguing sheds light on the wants and needs of others. Carl, even though you are frustrated with your wife and keep making her the butt of your jokes, you seem to want you marriage to work and are trying to get her to be less selfish and more responsible. Kelly, despite the fact that you continuously and purposely do things to rebel against your husband's wishes, you really want to be married to this 'old' man or you would have already left. You say you want this exciting and youthful life, but what you're really saying is that you're afraid that all of your best days are behind you.

"I want you both to think about what you want and need out of your life and marriage. Write it down if you have to. But when you both come here tomorrow, you are going to talk and make some decisions like adults who love each other and have loved each other well over a dozen years."

They both looked at me like I was crazy, but I expected that. I wasn't worried. I was certain that they had heard me and would do as I said. During session three, we would finally make some progress.

Franklin and Tamela. After much prayer about the Days, I decided the best method with them would be forwardness.

"Pastor and Lady Day," I said, once there were settled across from me on the sofa in the counseling office. "I want to be honest with you. Although your particular area of concern is not unusual for a couple your age, I am not completely qualified to counsel you on preparation for death. I typically work with people whose marriages are falling apart and they need some unbiased party to help them reconnect the dots. From time to time, I work with couples who have great marriages, but some internal or external issue is bothering one or both people and therefore adding stress to a solid marriage. But with you two, I'm not exactly sure how to approach counseling when both of you are certain of your relationship with God, so the issue is not being afraid of death or the afterlife. I guess what I'm saying is that you have six sessions with me, including this one, and we can talk about whatever you like during this time, but I may not be able to achieve as much with you as I hope to with the other couples at the retreat."

Franklin offered a warm smile. "Dr. Wilson, we appreciate your honesty. Maybe all we need is a place to just air out our thoughts about our mortality."

I felt relieved. Although telling a client that you couldn't help them was professionally the right thing to do, it was also hard to admit. I was grateful that they didn't appear disappointed and had offered a solution. "If that's what you need, I am totally here for you."

"Good," Franklin said. "And let's stay in prayer that whatever was meant to come out of our time here with you, will happen."

"Sounds like a plan." We spent the duration of the session discussing a few of their close friends that had recently died, and their experiences hearing the news and attending the funerals. By the end of our time, they both reported feeling lighter as if they had released some of the weight of their sadness. Maybe I would be more helpful to them than I thought.

Jordan and Sarah. Jordan appeared a little more comfortable the second session, and I could tell that he was beginning to acclimate to both counseling and South Beach. I figured that since Sarah was expressing concern about his anxiety and anger, it had to be causing strain in their marriage despite the fact that neither one of them had communicated this to me. So I just decided to take the straight forward approach and ask them.

"You've identified a desire to work on Jordan's anxiety and anger, yet I haven't heard anything about how his behavior impacts the marriage. Yes, I am sure that you both would love to see him find a way to have better control over his emotions, but I am also guessing that these uncontrolled emotions are causing a certain level of friction within the marriage, even if it's just periodically. Am I correct in my assumption?"

"Yeah," Sarah said, her eyes cast downward. "Sometimes, I just feel like we can't talk to each other without it becoming an argument."

Jordan didn't respond.

"Okay," I said. "So what I will do is recommend to you all a psychiatrist in your area to work one-on-one with Jordan. I will try to find someone who can offer both medication management and psychotherapy. Jordan will be assessed for whether or not he needs to be on a psychotropic medication such as anti-anxiety or anti-depression meds. He will also need to work with someone who can help him to learn to express and control his emotions in a healthy manner. This type of assistance is more long-term, so I won't even attempt to work with you all in that manner with the limited time we have here. What I do think that we can accomplish during these sessions is starting to discuss how his anxiety and anger affects your marriage, and how you all can implement some coping techniques and better communication skills to reduce the tension."

They both agreed to this game plan, and we spent the rest of the session talking about a few of the most memorable instances where his anger and anxiety caused a problem between them. From listening to their stories, I was relieved to gather that Jordan was not abusive toward his wife or child. In many cases of PTSD, aggression is projected onto family members. Jordan's anger was more internalized where he took it out on himself rather than his family. Still, his unhealthy emotional state impacted them as a unit because he often battled with depression, restlessness, verbal aggressiveness, and paranoia. Based on session two, I intended to teach them some basic couples' communication skills in our third meeting.

Martin and Lydia. I began my session with the Woods, having them talk about their emotional and mental experiences as they watched each of their children leave the home and move on to college. I wanted to let them get any thoughts or feelings about their journey thus far out in the open, so that as we continued in our work, we wouldn't be held back by unexpressed emotions.

Once they finished their story about their youngest child, I said, "Very good. Thank you for sharing your experiences with me. Now I would like to switch gears a bit and discuss your roles in life and the various hats that you wear. As people, we are multidimensional. We aren't just a mother or a father, but we are a wife, a husband, a business owner, an employee, and so on. In addition, even amongst those different roles, there are sub-roles that we play. For instance, Lydia, as a mother, you probably also have the sub-role of a cook, a cleaner, and prayer warrior, a provider, a comforter, an advocate, and so forth. The point that I'm trying to make is that there are many roles we play and that our roles are dependent on the situation and those around us. Are you all following me so far?"

They both nodded.

"Great. One of the major difficulties associated with empty nest syndrome is having an abrupt change in roles. Several months ago, you were expected to be a mother who fulfilled certain needs and performed various activities for your youngest daughter. When the two oldest left, you probably experienced a shift, but you were still able to continue in your parenting roles with your youngest. However, when Nicole left, your parenting hat had to change immediately. Nicole didn't need you in the same way anymore, and Martin Jr. and Alexis had already changed their relationship with you all when they left. With parenting, we get so used to being the people our children need us to be that when they leave, we don't know how to adjust ourselves to their changing needs, as well as go back to a position of focusing more on our spouse's and our own needs."

I gave them both a sheet of paper and pen which I already had laid to the side for their session, and said, "I want you to create two lists. On the front of this paper, I want you to write out all of the different roles that you played for your children when they were in your home. On the back, I want you to write down all of the roles that you are now playing for your children now that they are away. I also want you to indicate next to each role whether it is a high or low need for that role. For example, on both sides you may have cooking or cook, but on the first side you may write high to show that there was a great need for you to cook for your children when they were in grade school. Yet on the back, it may now be a low need to cook because you are only cooking for them when they come home on the weekends or holidays. I'm going to give you the remainder of the session to start working on this, and then you can take it with you and finish it tonight. We'll look at your lists and discuss them tomorrow."

I had my eyes closed as I mentally replayed the final moments of Martin and Lydia's session. Exhaling, I opened my eyes, startled to come face to face with my husband. I don't know how long he had been sitting in front of me, waiting for me to come out of my trance. He was aware of my after work download technique, so he must have decided to let me finish before getting my attention.

"Hey," I said.

"Hey," he responded.

"What are you doing out here?"

"I was just hanging out on the beach and I saw you sitting here."

"Oh." I looked away for a moment, now feeling ashamed about my behavior that morning. Neither of us spoke, we just allowed a few minutes of quiet to pass between us. Finally, I peered back at him and said, "Listen, Lem. I'm sorry for what I said earlier. I know it was foul. I was just upset, and I was being a brat. I apologize if I hurt your feelings."

He nodded. "Mmm. It was foul, but I messed up too, so I'm sorry too."

"So, we're cool?" I asked, relieved that we had buried the hatchet.

He smiled. "Yeah, we're cool."

Another silent minute passed. "I paid the mortgage."

"I know. I checked the account to see how much we owed and when was that latest that we could pay it, and I saw that it had been taken care of. Thanks."

"Yep."

"So, do you want to grab some dinner . . . together?" he asked.

"Sure. Why not?"

I stood up from my beach towel, brushed off a few specks of sand, rolled up the towel, and inserted it into my beach bag. We decided to make the restaurant selection easy on ourselves and eat at our hotel. While we waited for our food, I carried my bag upstairs to our room and slid my feet into a different pair of sandals—one's that didn't have grains of sand lodged in them. I was psyched when I got back down to the restaurant and noticed that our food had been served. We ate our meals while being entertained by live music and a Latin dancer performing on the patio. It felt good to be reconnected with Lem, and once again enjoying our time in Florida. After dinner, we headed down to the Clevelander which was a hotel that had an outdoor pool and party area. I hadn't danced with my husband in a long time, but we changed all of that by marching into the middle of the dance area and dusting off our signature two-step.

Two hours later, we emerged from the Clevelander, sweaty and out of breath. I threw my body down and hugged our bed the minute we walked into our hotel room. I tried to think back to the days when I could dance all night, but they seemed so long ago. Now I was certain that our 120 minutes of disco fever was going to cost me a sore body in the morning.

Lem crawled into bed with me, running his hands up and down my left arm. "That was fun, wasn't it?"

"That was awesome," I said. "I just wish I had some prescription pain medicine because I probably won't be able to walk tomorrow."

"That makes two of us."

We laughed.

It was quiet for a few minutes and then he asked, "Sweetheart, did you decide what you're going to do about your car payment this month?"

Although I didn't look up at him, I could feel his eyes on me. Why did he have to bring this topic up now? We were having such a great evening and I really didn't want to think about our financial woes.

I sighed. "No." I was afraid to ask, but I had to. Lem never asked a question unless there was a reason. "Why?"

"Nothing. Don't worry about it."

It was worse than I thought. If he was hesitant to tell me everything, it usually meant that there was something big that I was completely unaware of. I turned my body over and looked up at him, bracing myself for the impact of whatever it was. "Why, Lem? You may as well just tell me the truth because I'm going to find out anyway."

He stared at me with sad eyes. "My truck payment is due. It's actually behind two months. If I don't pay it, the bank is going to repossess it. I was hoping that you could help me with catching up on the truck if you were planning to wait to pay off your car until I got paid from this job."

I glared at him. I waited a few seconds, hoping he would laugh and say that he was just joking, but his face never changed. He was serious which made me heated. "What? You mean to tell me that not only did you give away our money, but you also haven't paid your car note in two months? What's going on, Lem? Why didn't you tell me this yesterday when we discussed everything?"

He backed away from me. I could see in his eyes that he wished he had never told me the truth. "Because you were already mad and I didn't want to make it worse. Andrea, you know me. You know that I'm not one of these lazy men that won't work and just want to live off a woman. I've work hard my entire life. In the five years that we've been married, I have always made sure that the bills were paid and that we had a roof over our heads. I'm just going through a dry spell with my business and I really need you to be there for me right now."

I let out a heavy sigh and shook my head in disbelief. "How much?"

"What?"

"How much are you asking for?" I asked again, angrily. I knew he heard my question the first time; he was just buying time.

He turned his eyes toward the TV although it wasn't on. "I need a grand."

I almost screamed. "One thousand dollars? Do I look like I'm made out of money?"

He glanced back at me. "Andrea, you know I would do it for you if the situation were reversed."

I sat up in the bed and rubbed my head which now was starting to ache. He was stressing me out. "The situation wouldn't be reversed because I would never be this irresponsible. How could you give all of your money away?"

His eyes widened. "I didn't give my money away. I paid my people for the work they did."

"No, you gave your money away," I said quickly. "You should have never accepted and finished a job without getting paid first. How many times have I told you this? And if you haven't gotten paid, why should your 'people' get paid? You should've told them before the job the agreement you made with the client, and if they wanted to work and take the risk, they would have to wait for the payment just like you. But noooooo. You're too busy acting like you're the man to be honest with your 'people' or to make your clients pay you upfront. How many times do we have to go through this before you get it through your thick skull that this is not the way to run a business? I'm not going to keep cleaning up your messes!"

"Andrea, don't act like you're so perfect. You've made bad choices too."

I rolled my eyes. "What? Like trusting you with our money?"

"You know what? You've got one more time to disrespect me before I—"

"Before you do what?" I challenged him.

He got out of the bed and headed to the corner of the room to retrieve his luggage. He slammed the suitcase on to the bed, then picked his cell phone up from the nightstand. "Forget it, Andrea. Forget I ever asked you for the money. You walk around here telling all these people how to save their marriages, but you're too selfish to save your own. So enjoy the rest of your little retreat, because I'm gone."

"Do what you have to do, Lem," I said, but my words didn't mimic my heart. I wasn't sure how we had gone from break dancing to breaking up, but my husband had said he was leaving, and for some reason, I wasn't stopping him. I knew I wasn't handling the problem like a professional, but at that moment, I wasn't a professional, I was an angry wife with a husband that was doing stupid stuff with our money. Every other woman in the world got their chance to be irate and emotional, and I wanted mine too. I was tired of being the perfect wife with the perfect marriage. It would be one thing if it were true, if we were really perfect, but the truth was that we had issues and struggles like everyone else. We just hid it better than others because we had to. Who in their right mind wanted marriage counseling by a psychologist whose marriage was just as bad as or maybe even worse than theirs? I loved my husband, but not enough to let him ruin all of our hard work with idiotic decisions that would leave us in the poor house. If that's where he wanted to end up, he could go there by himself because I wasn't letting him take me down in the process. Like the popular saying goes, "I could do bad all by myself." Didn't he know that money issues were one of the top reasons people got divorced? I know I'd told him this fact plenty of times. I needed him to pay attention.

I watched my husband pick up the phone and call the airline to switch his plane ticket to the first flight out the next morning. We traveled so much and had so many frequent flyer miles saved up that I wasn't worried about him affording a flight if necessary. As he waited for customer service to adjust his ticket, he began packing his suitcase, throwing clothes and shoes into it without any attempt to organize them.

Not wanting to witness my husband walking out on me, I jumped down off the bed, stomped into the bathroom, and jerked the door shut. I needed to take a shower. Hot water always calmed my nerves and helped me to think. As I turned on the shower, I heard the room door close. When I didn't hear any movement inside our room, I opened the bathroom door and poked my head into the room. Lem was gone, and so was his suitcase. I pushed my back against the door jam, slid down to the floor, and let out a heartbroken cry.

Lesson 9: Keep It One-Hundred

Stand therefore, having your loins girt about with truth, and having on the breastplate of righteousness. (Ephesians 6:14)

Eric

I didn't care what Dr. Wilson said, I needed some loving from my wife. What was the point of being married if I was going to burn with desire anyway? Amber and I had a wonderful afternoon on Sunday, hanging on the beach with Martin and Lydia. Who knew they could be so much fun? By the time evening rolled around, I just wanted to have a romantic dinner with my wife and enjoy a night of passion—just being honest. But *Dr. Wilson* had basically told Amber that it was okay for her to withhold her body from me. That wasn't Biblical! I knew the Bible and it clearly stated that a wife's body belonged to her husband and vice versa. Dr. Wilson needed to check her facts before she gave out bad advice.

So Amber and I have this perfect candlelight dinner at a restaurant on Ocean Drive and based on the way Amber was letting her hair down, I thought it would be a good time to try to cuddle with her. We get back to the hotel, get dressed for bed, and I attempt to pull my wife close.

Blocked.

Amber pushed me away like I was a third serving of Thanksgiving dinner. Seriously? I tried my approach again, this time starting by running my fingers through her hair. She'd always loved when I stroked her hair. She allowed me to caress her locks, but the moment my hand traveled down to her shoulders, she stiffened and pulled away.

"Stop, Eric," she murmured and slid the comforter higher to cover the shoulder I had just touched.

I was past frustrated. I was a grown man. I was a married man. I had a right to touch my wife's shoulder or any other part of her body that I wanted.

"Amber," I pleaded. "Let me just hold you."

"Un unn." She shot me down. "Go to sleep."

"I don't want to go to sleep. I want to get some attention from my wife."

"Eric, we already discussed this in counseling. I'll let you know when I'm ready, but it won't be tonight."

"Why not?"

"Because I'm not ready. Dr. Wilson said we need to wait until I'm ready."

I wasn't someone who used foul language, but at that moment, I almost slipped. "Forget Dr. Wilson. I'm not married to Dr. Wilson, I'm married to you. What she told us isn't even right. The Bible says that your body belongs to me. She doesn't even know what she's talking about."

"Yes, she does, Eric. You agreed in her office. Why are you acting stupid now?"

"She doesn't have an office. It's a hotel room which is exactly my point. We're getting counseling in a hotel room. That should be a sign that we should be making love. How can I focus during counseling when there's a bed in the room and I haven't had any in months?"

"Eric, that doesn't even make sense. Go to bed because you're talking crazy."

"I'm not talking crazy; I'm being serious. A man has needs, Amber. You need to handle your wifely duties."

Amber sucked her teeth. "You need to go to sleep because this conversation is over."

"Amber, you're not being fair. There are all of these half-naked women in bikinis on South Beach, showing all kinds of legs and cleavage and you won't even let me hug you. How am I supposed to feel?"

"What are you trying to say, Eric? Are you implying that you want to cheat? That you want one of these women out here?"

"No, that's not what I'm saying. Don't twist my words. I'm just telling you that you're not making this easy for me."

"It's not easy for me either, Eric. So, you're okay with us having sex even though I am telling you that it hurts me? That doesn't sound like love."

I huffed. "I don't know what you expect from me."

"I expect you to honor my decision and be understanding."

"I understand alright. I understand that you won't even try. It has been three months! How do you know that it will be painful when you won't even try?"

"Because I know."

"No, you don't. Stop being stubborn."

"Kick rocks, Eric."

"Eat glue, Amber."

"Yo' momma, Eric."

I didn't even respond to her, because had I responded, my likely smart aleck would have led to an even bigger argument than we were already having. It was fruitless. She wasn't budging and the more I begged her, the more annoyed I became about the whole situation. Instead, I crawled back to my edge of the bed and sulked myself to sleep, cursing Dr. Wilson in my mind the entire time.

Monday morning, we dragged ourselves to sunrise prayer, both of us looking like someone put spoiled milk in our coffee. I looked around at the other couples, and found a twinge of solace in the fact that Carl and Kelly seemed just as crabby as Amber and I. Even Dr. Wilson appeared a bit disheveled, and surprisingly, her husband, who had attended all of the sunrise prayer meetings up until that point, was missing. However, I didn't think much of it because I knew they had a different reason for being at the retreat than the rest of us. More than likely, he was free to participate as he pleased.

The prayer session whizzed by as Amber and I broke off into our private space on the beach and prayed in silence. I found myself asking God to change Amber's heart and mind about sex, and to heal her from whatever ailment was keeping her from allowing us to be intimate. I hated that this one issue was driving a serious wedge between us. I felt like a madman or pervert, constantly asking her to let me get close to her. But I wasn't some nymphomaniac, I was just a man who craved physical affection. What was wrong with that?

Amber decided to skip breakfast, as well as Kelly, so Carl and I sat together at the restaurant in front of the hotel directly after prayer. It was somewhat of a relief to have some time away from my wife, especially with all of the tension between us. I suspected Carl felt the same because he seemed to deflate the minute Kelly left his presence.

"Is it *that* bad?" I asked, as we waited for our food.

Carl glanced across the table at me and shook his head. "What do you think?"

"I've never seen you look so stressed out. You're always the upbeat one."

"That was until my wife regressed into a 15-year-old. Imagine if Amber all of a sudden started acting like she was twelve? How *upbeat* would you be?"

I laughed. "Every time you talk about Kelly, she gets younger and younger. By the end of today, she'll be a newborn."

Carl sighed. "Sometimes that's what it feels like. I just never thought we'd be going through this. After all of our ups and downs, I thought we had gotten to this place where we had worked out most of the kinks in our marriage. If we were going to be arguing, I imagined that it would be over something that makes sense like which college to send the girls to or where to go on a second honeymoon, not whether or not her skirt is too short or if a married woman should be at the bar all night. I just don't get it."

"Yeah, that has to be rough. I hope Amber never tries to stick her foot in the fountain of youth."

Carl chuckled. "Nah, Amber's not like that. You've got a good woman. She can be a firecracker at times, but she means well. Plus she's softened up a lot since you two have been married. Remember when she was single and used to come into the office angry after a bad date or a business meeting. Man! I hated those days. I used to be like I'm going out to show a house before she starts rolling her neck at me."

I laughed again. "Yeah, she was a trip. What am I talking about? She still is a trip. I love that woman, but sometimes she can be meaner than a junkyard dog."

Two curvaceous women strolled past the table wearing bikini tops and denim cutoff shorts. Both Carl and I ceased our conversation and gawked at the women until they were out of our view. Carl was the first to look away and therefore caught me staring at the attractive females.

"What are you doing?" he asked, causing me to return my focus to our table.

"Huh? Nothing."

He smiled at me as if he were unconvinced. "E, I saw that. You were checking out those cuties. That's not your style. Something must be going on with you and Amber. What's up, man?"

"So because I looked twice at another woman, you figure there's something wrong with my marriage? And you looked, too," I reminded him.

"Yeah, I looked," he admitted. "One, something *is* wrong in my marriage, and two, I *always* look. But you usually don't look so I know there's a problem. Whatever it is, more than likely I've been there and done that. When are you going to learn that I'm your boy? I've got your back."

I wanted to tell Carl, but intimacy issues are not something you walk around telling folks. "I'm a little embarrassed to say."

"Come on, E. My wife is at the club every night acting like she just hit puberty. What's more embarrassing than that?"

"We're not . . . you know?" I said, my voice barely louder than a whisper.

Carl leaned in. "No, I don't know. You're not what?"

I looked around to make sure the coast was clear. When I was sure that my wife wasn't in the vicinity, I said, "Amber and I are not having sex."

"What?" Carl said loudly. "Even since you've been in Miami?"

"Nope. And keep your voice down," I said, hushing him.

Carl grinned. It annoyed me that he was finding pleasure in my pain. "Dude, that's messed up. I've got a wannabe 8-year-old for a wife and we still do the do. Are you the problem because we can get you some—"

I cut him off. "No, I'm not the problem. I don't need any-thing," I said, making the word anything sound like two words instead of one. "I'm ready. It's her. She doesn't want to anymore. With the miscarriages and everything, she just stopped. She really wants a baby, Carl, but I don't know how she thinks she's going to have one if we don't even touch anymore."

"Man, E. Okay, I have to tell you. That's a new one for me. Kelly might try to put the goodies on lockdown every once in a while when she's mad at me, but we've never just stopped completely. How long has this been going on? Please tell me only a few weeks."

"Three months."

"Dog! You've got to be kidding me."

"Carl, you're not making me feel any better."

"My bad. I just didn't think it was that bad. I don't know what I'd do if Kelly cut me off like that. And we're down here with all of these hot women too."

"I know," I said, eagerly. "That's what I tried to tell her. She's killing me, literally. I'm dying."

Carl laughed at my dramatics, then asked, "Is this the issue you all are talking to Dr. Wilson about? What did she say?"

"You were right, Carl. She sided with Amber. Told me to refrain from touching Amber until she's ready. That could be forever! I can't wait that long. I don't even know if I can last another day. It was one thing when I was single, but when you're married and you've got this beautiful woman that you love lying in the bed right next to you every night, it's straight torture."

Carl whistled. "Wow, I feel for you. Just try to hold on, my brother. And stay away from the beach in the meantime. These women out here are killing the game! I've never had so many lustful thoughts in my life. That sunrise prayer and those classes are the only things keeping me from falling straight into temptation. The Woods didn't lie. They put us right in the middle of the lion's den."

A sense of panic spread across my chest. Our issues seemed magnified in Miami. A new question burned in my mind. *How would we all survive South Beach?*

The time in between prayer and the couples' class also speed by, and I found myself feeling relieved to go to the couples' class. My talk with Carl only amplified the war within me. Our conversation mixed with the silent treatment Amber had given me all morning had me both flustered and fearful, and I sincerely hoped that something the Woods had prepared for us would help us to pull our marriage back into perspective. I was grateful that Martin led that day's class. Although I felt that Lydia was an excellent teacher, Martin always used masculine examples to break down the material that I could really relate to.

"It's Day Three, everyone," Martin began. "Let's recap. So far we have called out and identified that our enemies are the powers of evil, and that we must come to the battle with spiritual armor, prepared to fight. Today we will discuss what I believe is one of the most difficult lessons you will receive during this bootcamp. Let's begin by reading the scripture."

He opened his Bible. "Ephesians 6:14 says, 'Stand therefore—hold your ground—having tightened the belt of truth around your loins and having put on the breastplate of integrity and moral rectitude and right standing with God.' I believe that this lesson is one of the harder ones because today we are dealing with truth and righteousness, two concepts that seem foreign in today's society.

"In verse fourteen, there are two different spiritual items that we are encouraged to wear to war. The first is the belt of truth and the second is the breastplate of righteousness or right standing with God. Let's start with the second item, the breastplate of righteousness."

Martin put down his Bible and placed his hands over his chest. "The breastplate is a piece of armor designed to protect a soldier from his neck to his gut. The majority of the major organs that we need to survive are located in our mid-section which the breastplate covers. Our heart, lungs, stomach, kidneys, and liver are all within this region of our body. Therefore shielding this area is vital during battle.

"Righteousness is right standing with God. It's decency, virtue, honor, and having morals. Having these traits can safeguard our spiritual heart, lungs, stomach, kidney, and liver, especially during spiritual warfare. What this means is that your values, your morals, your right standing with God keeps the enemy from hurting or destroying your heart—how you feel and how you love; your lungs—your ability to breathe in life and to receiving fresh air; your stomach—how you digest and take in the fuel you need to sustain yourself; your kidneys and liver—how you process both the good and bad stuff that comes into your system. Without righteousness, all of these functions are vulnerable and at risk of failure. Don't let the devil trick you into giving up your morals and values. It could cost you your life in this spiritual battle."

Martin's words were exactly what I needed to hear. I wasn't planning to cheat on Amber, but my ability to maintain decent and righteous thoughts had been dwindling. I would have to fight with all of my might to keep my mind on God and doing the right thing, not allowing my flesh or the scantily dressed women on South Beach to lead me astray.

Martin picked up his Bible. "Now let's go back to the first item listed in the verse, the belt of truth. In order to understand this piece of equipment, we should consider what a belt is used for in the physical realm. Now some of us just wear a belt as a fashion statement. I see some of the younger women putting a belt on top of their shirts or dresses, but it really has no functionality. However, a belt was created initially to hold up a person's pants. The way pants are made, depending on the person wearing them and the size of the pants, the pants may easily fall down if one is not wearing a belt. In most cases, both the person wearing the pants and those around them do not want to experience or witness their bottoms falling down. Often, many people get upset with young people for sagging their pants because it is improper to expose one's underwear to the world. There is a reason we call it underwear—it should be worn under the clothes and not exposed for all to see. So it is the physical belt that keeps one together, unexposed, from falling apart, proper and appropriate."

Martin pointed to the brown leather belt that held up his khaki shorts. "In old school battle gear, the belt was also the place where a solider would keep his sword. It was important for the belt to be included in the military regalia because without it, the solider would have no place to store his sword during times when he didn't need it or needed his hands freed to accomplish another task.

"Considering the physical function of a belt, we can relate it to its purpose in God's armor. The spiritual belt, the item that is needed to keep us spiritually together, unexposed, from falling apart, proper and appropriate, and freed up, is truth. When we decide to wear the belt of truth, we are choosing a spiritual article of clothing that will protect us from falling apart, it keeps us together during battle, it keep us from being exposed in an improper manner or vulnerable to our enemy, and it keeps us free as long as we wear and use it."

He shook his Bible at us as if reprimanding a child. "Many of us aren't wearing our spiritual belts of truth. We're not keeping it one-hundred percent like the young people say. We're not being honest with ourselves and our spouses. We're pretending that we are somebody that we aren't. We are deceitful, liars, fakers, pretenders, and omiters of the truth. And then we wonder why our families are falling apart. We don't understand why we are constantly vulnerable and being attacked by the enemy. We don't have freedom in our lives and we always feel something is in the way of us being able to be freed up to do what we were called to do, and to have what God has promised. Maybe it's because we're not wearing the belt of truth. It's time we let go of the lies, put on the truth, and kept it one-hundred."

I looked over at Amber whose face appeared ashen as if she had just seen a ghost. We had counseling with Dr. Wilson next. I prayed that she had heard Martin's words of wisdom and was finally ready to stop playing games and keep it real with both me and herself.

Lesson 10: A Time to Weep

A time to weep, and a time to laugh; a time to mourn, and a time to dance. (Ecclesiastes 3:4)

Verily, verily, I say unto you, That ye shall weep and lament, but the world shall rejoice: and ye shall be sorrowful, but your sorrow shall be turned into joy. (John 16:20)

Amber

No, Eric did not try to weasel himself onto my side of the bed! Did he or did he not hear Dr. Wilson tell him to respect my wishes not be touched until I was ready? What part of I'm not ready didn't he understand? Yes, we had a great day together, but that didn't mean having sex was the natural thing to do next. Why couldn't he just chill?

Please know that I did not enjoy making my husband suffer. I knew he was on the verge of pulling his hair out. I actually felt sorry for him. The people pleasing part of me wanted to give in and give him the goodies at least once to help take the edge off. Yet, memories of our last few times and how much sex ached always nipped that idea in the bud.

Eric continued to pester me until I had to get mean and I hated being mean to him. Since the Wife 101 course, I had tried to be kind and gentle towards him. It wasn't easy and often my former bad attitude snuck back in and won out over goodness. Afterwards, I would repent to God, apologize to my husband, and remind myself of my goal to be a better woman. I was slowly getting there, but I had a long way to go. A long, long way.

The next morning, having to pray with him was awkward. How do you earnestly pray with and for someone who is rocking your nerves? I pushed past my irritation and his foul mood, and prayed anyways, asking God to help us because we desperately needed divine intervention. I decided to skip breakfast and lounge in bed a little longer, so I left Eric with his buddy Carl, figuring they could entertain themselves. Besides, that morning, I was certain that he preferred Carl's company more than mine.

After catching a nearly two-hour nap, I reluctantly pulled myself out of the bed and headed to the couples' class. Martin must have been talking to God about me because his message hit me upside the head like a cast iron skillet. I had always considered myself an honest person, sometimes to a fault, but when it came to my feelings about sex and my unborn babies, I hadn't been as upfront with my husband as I should have. I didn't want to deal with the heartbreak I felt about my weak womb or the bitterness I felt about him already having a child. I could empathize with Hannah from the book of 1 Samuel, who just wanted a child with her husband, and had to stomach her husband's other wife Peninnah who had a bunch of children and bragged about it on purpose. Lena was my Peninnah, and although she wasn't technically married to Eric and hardly said two words to me, her presence alone, along with that of her daughter, was a constant reminder of my shortcomings. But I hadn't told Eric about my perspective because he would think I was being silly, and he would probably misunderstand my feelings about Jonelle. I loved Jonelle, but my care for her didn't override my jealousy over her. So I held back these brutalizing thoughts and emotions. It seemed like the right choice, but with one powerful message delivered by Martin Woods, I began to feel guilty and exposed.

Sitting next to Eric on the sofa in Dr. Wilson's office, I knew in my heart that I had to reveal what I wished I could keep hidden forever. I wondered how Dr. Wilson would interpret my confession, and if she would still back me up about not having sex once I spilled my secret. I looked up at her, trying to gauge her opinion of me, but I couldn't get a sense of her energy. She didn't come off as warm as she had the day prior, but maybe that was just my own insecurities creating reasons to avoid telling the truth. Nevertheless, it was now or never.

Before we could get too deep into the session, I spoke up. "I need to say something."

Dr. Wilson looked at me as if she couldn't care less, yet said, "Okay. Go ahead."

"I was listening to Minister Martin talk today about keeping it one-hundred and I feel like the message was for me. It's not that I haven't been truthful about what's been discussed so far, but I do have some thoughts and feelings that I haven't expressed yet."

Eric looked at me like he was confused. Dr. Wilson nodded and said, "Please share."

I rubbed my hands together. "Well," I sighed. "When you asked me if I blame Eric or myself about my babies dying, I said no. And I really don't, at least I don't think that I do. But even though I know it's not either of our faults, I do feel resentful about it."

I stalled a bit and Dr. Wilson glared at me as if she was becoming impatient. "How so?" she probed.

I was sensing a little hostility from her, despite the semi smile that remained plastered on her face. I guess I couldn't be mad about it because if I were in her shoes, I would be getting annoyed with me too. I said I had something to say, so I needed to go on and say it, and stop playing around. I cleared my throat, swallowed the small lump that indicated that tears were nearby, and willed myself to be courageous. "I resent the fact that Eric already has a child with someone else, but doesn't have one with me. I resent the fact that Lena, Eric's daughter's mother, gets to play a role in his life that I don't get to play. I resent the fact that there are unfit mothers out there who abuse their children and abort their kids, and I can't even have one." I felt hot tears begin to stream down my face, but I was on a roll and wouldn't stop confessing until I had let it all out. "I resent the fact that Eric's daughter has a part of his heart that I can't have, that he loves her more than he loves me, and that the only way that I can even get close to that part of him is to have a child with him which obviously, I ca . . . I ca . . . I can't. I can't have his babies," I sobbed. "I don't know why. I haven't been perfect, but I did everything right with Eric. We abstained from sex until we were married. I waited until I could afford to have a child. We have everything a baby could need. We're ready, but I can't. I'm the problem. How could this happen? How could God let this happen? I wish He would just take the desire away from me if I can't have it."

I bowed my head and covered my eyes with my hands, feeling ashamed of the words I had just spoken. Two sets of eyes were gazing at me; I could feel their intensity even with my head lowered. The room became quiet—outside of my sniffles. I really hated how Dr. Wilson was comfortable with silence. It seemed like she purposely didn't speak at an emotional moment just to rile us up more. I looked up at both of them. "Say something!" I demanded, feeling like a fool for pouring out my heart and not getting an immediate response.

I thought I saw Dr. Wilson subtly roll her eyes, but maybe I was just imagining it. She directed her attention to Eric and asked, "Do you have a response for Amber?"

Eric shook his head. "I don't know what to say."

His lack of feedback was like a knife to my stomach. I crumpled over in pain, releasing more sorrowful tears.

Dr. Wilson let me cry for maybe thirty seconds, before she addressed me. "Amber, although counseling is not about me providing the answers, but you—the client—coming up with your own solutions, there are times when a therapist will speak frankly about a situation. This is one of those moments. Based on all that you've said both today and since we've begun these session, I don't believe there is anything physically wrong with you that is causing the pain you're experiencing during sex."

"But I'm not lying. It hurts!" I said, feeling defensive.

"I am not saying that sex doesn't hurt. It probably does, but not because there is something *physically* wrong with you. The body, mind, and spirit are not isolated components, they are interconnected. Therefore what affects the mind, impacts the body and spirit. You stated that you waited until marriage to engage in a sexual relationship with your husband. Sex then represents your commitment to him and the building of a family. However, you've been unable to carry a child to term, and Eric does not solely belong to you. He has a commitment outside of you by having a child that is not yours. As you just said, you resent the position you are in. I believe the bitterness you feel is what is causing the pain during sex. For women, sex is mostly psychological, so if you're mentally connecting sex to your disappointment, frustration, and anger about your miscarriages, it would make sense that your body would reject intimacy, keeping you from enjoying sex, and maybe even cause intercourse to be painful."

I glanced over at Eric who still appeared to be overwhelmed about my confession. The moment our eyes met, he looked away from me and turned his attention to Dr. Wilson.

"So what you're saying is that all of these negative emotions Amber has built up about me is the reason that she won't have sex with me?" Eric asked.

"Probably. But the negative emotions aren't just toward you, Eric. They are also toward herself and most likely God. Anyone she sees as a threat to her happiness could be included. You need to know that it's not about you; it's about her accepting that sometimes life isn't fair and we all have to deal with our shattered dreams."

Amber sniffled. "If what you're saying is true, that this is a completely psychological issue, what do I have to do to overcome it?"

"If what I'm *suggesting* is true, you will have to forgive, make amends, and let go. You'll have to come to terms with the idea that children may not be a part of the plan for your life, and being a stepmother may be your version of motherhood. You will have to make peace with God, your husband, and yourself, and let yourself feel loved again. There's no magic wand or pill to make everything okay. You just have to want it bad enough to work through the pain."

Lesson 11: A Time to Hate

A time to love and a time to hate, a time for war and a time for peace. (Ecclesiastes 3:8)

The fear of the LORD is to hate evil: pride, and arrogance, and the evil way, and the perverse mouth, do I hate. (Proverbs 8:13)

Dr. Wilson

Okay, here's the truth. I hated my husband—at least that was the thought that kept circling my mind. Lem had left me solo on a marriage retreat where I was supposed to be operating as a relationship expert. The predicament was two-fold. One, my marriage was in crisis. This was a crucial time when we really needed to work through the problem before it became unsolvable. His departure only magnified the issue because not only was both he and I vulnerable to acting out of anger, but he had also put me in a jam when it came to my job—which was the second part of the dilemma. The attendees of the marriage retreat knew that I was in South Beach with my husband. How was I going to explain his disappearance without lying or revealing to the group that I had bigger marital issues than all of them combined? Maybe not bigger, but just as problematic.

On Monday morning, I dragged myself to sunrise prayer even though I had no mate to pray with. I figured that if nothing else, I needed to be praying—hard. Since the start of the retreat, I had enjoyed the prayer time on the beach each morning. It really gave me the sensation of being at one with God through nature. When I arrived with no Lem in tow, a couple of the participants did a double-take, but no one said a word. I was hoping they thought he just slept in. Technically, neither he nor I were mandated to attend this activity.

When we broke off into pairs, I went to the spot where Lem and I usually prayed. I sat down on the cool sand and gazed out at the water. Just like I did with my client sessions, I reviewed my mental tape of the night prior's events leading up to Lem's departure. I had to admit, I'd played my part in our fight, yet I still didn't see myself as the one who was wrong. Nonetheless, it didn't matter whose fault it was. From my training and experience, I knew that marital success wasn't about pointing the finger of blame, but remaining focused on the ultimate goal— making the marriage work. As I had asked couples time and time again, would you rather be right or be married?

Since I was supposed to be praying, I did. But instead of the asking-for-my-wants sort of prayer, I simply talked to God about the situation.

"God, what am I supposed to do?"

I waited, as if I expected Him to answer me right away in a loud thunderous voice.

"I want my husband to be more responsible. I want to be able to trust him. I thought I could trust him, but now I see that he thinks it's okay to make decisions without me about issues that affect me. The worst part is that now I am expected to clean up his mess, and if I don't, then I'm a bad wife. And God, it's not even so much about money as it is about him not valuing how hard I work to help build a better life for us. It's like he thinks that because I have some money saved up that he should be able to use it as he pleases, forgetting that I saved the money for a reason. I'm not just holding on to money; I'm trying to make sure we reach our goals. How will we ever get anywhere if we are not good stewards of what's been given to us?"

What does it profit a man to gain the whole world yet lose his soul?

Huh? That was God's response? First of all, my soul wasn't in jeopardy—I didn't think. And second of all, was God really taking Lem's side?

Heat rose up in my neck and face. Here I was, trying to do the right thing, and now my soul was at risk because I didn't want to give all of my money away to pay for Lem's mistakes? I know you're not supposed to question God, but at that moment, I had some questions. Instead of asking them, I dismissed the small voice that was telling me that I was wrong, and promptly ended prayer time.

I went back to my room and took a two-hour long nap in an attempt to catch up from all of the sleep I was missing at night. When the alarm went off at 9:45 a.m., I grumbled, "Bah humbug," and forced myself up and out the door for the couples' class.

Of course Martin had to teach about righteousness and truth. Thanks, God, for rubbing it in. I sat through the class, pretending not to hear the message which seemed intentionally aimed at me. Although I wasn't in the mood to counsel anyone, I was relieved when Martin dismissed us and I was able to head back to the hotel for my sessions. In my mind, I plotted out how I would tolerate my first two couples—Eric/Amber and Carl/Kelly—who were my most troubled clients, grab a quick burger from Johnny Rockets for lunch, see if I could catch a thirty-minute nap, then breeze through the last three couples, order dinner to go from the Beacon's restaurant, and lock myself in my room for the rest of the evening. It sure sounded like a good plan to me.

By 6:00 p.m., I was lying on my back in the middle of my room's king-sized bed, stuffed from dinner, and allowing the counseling sessions to roll through my mind. Since Lem was no longer with me, I skipped the beach self-debriefing and went straight for dinner. But now that I had eaten, I was fully aware that I would not be able to relax for the night if I didn't go through my routine of letting go of my day. So I took a deep breath and mentally ran through my sessions.

Eric and Amber. I guess I wasn't the only one who was impacted by Martin's teachings on righteousness and truth. Amber finally came clean on her conflicting emotions about her husband and her inability to have a baby. I knew from the moment that I saw her initial questionnaire that she was harboring bitterness, but I just couldn't come flat out and say it. No, it was my job to let her come to terms with her own struggles in her own time. I was glad that she found the courage to tell Eric how she really felt. I was wondering how long her innocent charade was going to last. I'm certain that she picked up on my waning patience. She was a lot like me, so I understood her more than she realized. But the difference between Amber and I was that Amber still believed in fairytales. She had this ideal vision of what life and marriage should be, and she attempted to make everyone around her fit into her box. With the loss of her children, life was teaching her that we always don't get what we want, and that sometimes, the beauty could be found in the imperfections. Eric looked as if he had been hit by a train, especially when Amber admitted to feeling resentful about his daughter. She probably wouldn't have to worry about him touching her anytime soon. I probably should have shown more empathy, but I was having a bad day and couldn't seem to shake off my impassive disposition, which was exactly why I hated my husband for putting me in such a terrible position.

Carl and Kelly. My grumpiness and their craziness just didn't mixed. I begged, "Jesus, please help me," a few times before and during their time. There was no way that I could have sat through another spar session between them, although some of the jabs were quite comical. So I steered them in a different direction.

"Kelly, what was your life like before you got married?" I asked.

She shrugged. "It was cool. I hung out with my girls, went out from time to time, stuff like that."

"Why did you decide to get married?"

"I met Carl and we hit it off. I was in my twenties, but I wanted a family and I didn't want to be alone forever. I knew Carl would treat me right and be a good father, so when he asked me to marry him, I did."

I could see Carl squirming in his seat as if he had something to say, yet I kept my attention on Kelly. "So you wanted a family. Did that turn out the way you hoped?"

"In some ways, yes. In other ways, no. It was harder than I thought becoming a wife and a mom. I used to have a lot of fun when I was single, but then I had to grow up quick and get serious about everything. At first, Carl was still a bit immature, so I felt like I had to be strong for the both of us. It was a lot to adjust to, but we made it."

"And your friends, the ones that you used to hang with, are they still single?"

Kelly nodded. "Some of them. A couple of my girls got married, but there are still several of them that are single."

"Do you hang out with them?"

"No, not so much with the married ones because they are always with their families. But the ones who are single, yeah, we get together regularly."

She was being extremely honest, so I figured I would go in for the kill. "Kelly, do you envy your single friends in any way?"

She bit her bottom lip. After a few seconds, she said, "Sometimes. They all complain about being single and say they want to be like me, but I try to tell them that being married isn't all it's cracked up to be. I mean, I know that I'm blessed to have a good husband and healthy kids, but sometimes I look at my single friends and how carefree they are, and I just wish I would have waited longer before starting a family."

I nodded and finally turned my face toward Carl who was so anxious to speak that he looked as if he would burst. "Carl, how does hearing what your wife have to say make you feel?"

Carl inched toward the edge of his seat, seemingly glad to get his turn to talk. "Well, I appreciate her saying that her family is a blessing and that I'm a good husband because she neither tells me so nor does she act like it. I guess I understand how she feels to a certain extent because sometimes I get tired of all of the responsibility of having a family too. But just because I feel tired, that doesn't mean that it's okay to give up or act like my family should just disappear. This is the choice that I made, and this is what I have to deal with. I think she should do the same. Not only that, but there's a reason why her single friends want to be married so bad, because partying and hanging out gets old after a while. Eventually, we all have to grow up and take responsibility. No one gets a time-out from real life."

"I know what choice I made," Kelly responded.

"Then act like it," Carl said.

"I have!" Kelly exploded. "For almost twelve years I've been the faithful wife and mother, doing everything I can to make you and the girls lives happy. Don't I deserve to be happy too?"

"I've never held you back from being happy. I just don't want you to jeopardize our marriage and the image our daughters have of you by trying to relive your glory days."

Kelly rubbed her hands over her face as if flustered. I took it as a cue for me to intervene. "Okay, let me review what I've heard so far. Kelly, you've said that you do in fact want your family, but also feel as if the responsibility of having a family keeps you from feeling happy. Carl, you said that you can relate to Kelly's feelings, but don't want the way she feels to negatively impact the family. Am I correct?"

They both nodded.

"Okay, I am going to offer my perspective, and then I am going to give you two an assignment. I know that often we all get caught up in this idea of being happy. However, the Bible never promised us happiness. It promises us peace and even joy, but not happiness. Why? Because happiness is based on a temporary state. We are happy when situations in our lives are going according to the way we want. Yet the minute the situation changes, our ability to be happy also changes. So instead of aiming for happiness, aim for joy and peace. Both joy and peace are gifts that God can give you that have nothing to do with your situation. You can be going through the worst moments in life and still experience joy and peace.

"Now for your assignment, I want you both to write down your outlets. An outlet is an activity that makes your feel good, something you can do when you need a break to help you recoup. I also want you to write down the responsibilities in your home that stress you out the most. Bring both of these list in with you tomorrow and we'll go over them together."

Yes, I loved to give out homework and I enjoyed having my clients create lists. When they actually followed through, it was a great way to give them something tangible to reflect on. Feelings and thoughts weren't tangible, and because people couldn't see them, they were often hard to work with. But by having clients write down and look at their own thoughts and emotions, it was like helping them to see their problems in a more manageable light. Carl and Kelly agreed to the assignment and I felt a sense of true accomplishment with them for the first time since the retreat began, despite my less than perfect mood.

Franklin and Tamela. I was in a better place emotionally by the time I started working with the Days. After eating and taking a thirty minute power nap, I felt less sullen. Plus my progress with my first two couples of the day empowered me, leading me to believe that I could do my job well in the midst of a personal crisis.

My session with the Days again was more open in nature, allowing them to speak freely about fond memories of loved one and the reality of their mortality. Toward the end of the session, I was a little thrown off by Franklin saying to me, "I understand that you are here to counsel us, but please feel free to let us know if there is anything that we can do for you."

That was strange. I'd never had a client say something to me like that. Although I was taken aback by his comment, I quickly equated it to being a natural inclination with him being a pastor and all. "Thanks. I appreciate your concern," I said in response.

"We're serious," Tamela added. "We know this time is for us to talk about ourselves, but we don't mind sharing our time with you. We do a lot of counseling with couples at the church and we know the burden of having to carry others problems. It can sometimes even affect one's own marriage. So, if there is anything, anything at all, please know that we are here for you."

I offered them the most sincere smile that I could muster up and nodded in agreement. That was really weird. Had they been watching me? Could they see the glint of sadness in my eyes? Had they noticed Lem's disappearance? Or were they just a caring pastor and first lady who frequently offered a shoulder to any and every one they met. I didn't have an answer and I wasn't going to ask at the risk of exposing my own marital problems. Instead, I thought no more of their proposition and continued on like the professional that I was.

Jordan and Sarah. I didn't waste any time during my session with Jordan and Sarah. I immediately started teaching them communication skills.

"If we were at my office in New York, I would officially teach you Couples Communication. But since I don't have my mats and materials, I will teach you some of the basics," I said to Jordan and Sarah. "First, you must understand the difference between what is said versus how you say it. If information is said in the proper way, it is easier for your spouse to receive it. But when we don't communicate properly, our words are often rejected or misunderstood. You all following me so far?"

They both nodded.

"In Couples Communication, the message is broken up into five aspects of The Awareness Wheel—sensory data, thoughts, feelings, wants, and actions. The Awareness Wheel is basically a mat you would step on that has a circle with these five sections listed to help you communicate effectively. Today I am going to go over the first three areas. Sensory data is what you gather with your senses—what you see, hear, touch, taste, and smell. You start off communication by describing sensory data. For example, if the issue is that Sarah is upset because Jordan never wants to go out to dinner, Sarah might say, 'Jordan, I hear you tell me that you don't want to go out to dinner. I see us eating at home every night. I see me having to cook a lot since we eat at home every night.' After communicating all of your sensory data, you can move on to your thoughts. This is where it gets tricky. A lot of people mistake their thoughts for feelings and vice versa. A thought is an idea while a feeling is an emotion. So I don't *think* I am angry, I *feel* that I am angry. Or I don't *feel* you're not listening to me, I *think* you're not listening to me. You get it?"

Again they nodded.

"So you first begin with your thoughts about the issue. Sarah might say, 'I think we should go out to eat every once in a while. I think I deserve a break from cooking. I think it would be romantic to go out to eat. I think we should participate in more social activities like going out for dinner.' From there you move on to feelings. 'I feel unappreciated when you don't take me out. I feel sad that we don't do things in public anymore. I feel frustrated with always having to cook.' If at any point, you come up with a new thought, feeling, or sensory data, you must make sure to begin it in the correct manner, separating your thoughts, feelings, and sensory data. Understand?"

They nodded for the third time. It was good enough for me. I had them practice with a real issue in their relationship. They decided to use Jordan's tendency to withdrawal when he feels sad or angry. Both of them were able to adequately communicate using the three areas about the issue before the session ended. I planned to move onto the fourth aspect of The Awareness Wheel in the next session.

Martin and Lydia. I always felt a sense of peace by the time I got to my session with the Woods. My tranquility was probably a result of their calm-like demeanors mixed with the fact that they were my last couple of the day. Martin and Lydia came to the session prepared, having completed their role lists. I loved them even more for doing their homework on-time. I can't tell you how many couples claimed they wanted to work on their marriages, but couldn't find the time to finish any assignment I gave them. Their unwillingness to complete their homework revealed their lack of commitment to the process of bettering their marriage. But this was not the case with the Woods.

I listened closely as Lydia shared her lists with us. "My first list—roles I had while the kids were in the home—includes cook, maid, homework helper, chauffeur, prayer warrior, listener, advisor, affection giver, cheerleader, nurse, spiritual guide, shopper, bill manager, advocate, and role model. My second list— roles I currently have now that the kids are gone—is basically the same except I'm no longer a chauffeur, nurse, or homework helper, and now I'm less of a cook, maid, and shopper."

"Good job," I said to Lydia. "Martin, let's hear your list."

"Alright," said Martin. "Some of my past roles are the same as Lydia's and some are different. I have disciplinarian, spiritual head, breadwinner, advisor, advocate, encourager, money manager, role model, chauffeur, playmate, protector, and leader. My current roles are the same expect for no longer being a chauffeur, playmate or disciplinarian. I do less advocating and protecting. I also feel like I've started to become somewhat of a friend, at least to my oldest, my son."

"Me too, but with the girls," Lydia added.

"Both of you have done an excellent job with your lists and I applaud you for taking on the assignment. As you can see, although some of your roles with your children have changed, some have remained the same, the intensity has just changed because your kids are more independent. But that doesn't mean that they still don't need you to continue to play essential background positions in their lives like praying for them and guiding them. In addition, you've also gained a new role that you didn't have before and that is being a friend. When kids are minors, it's hard to be friends with them because you need to play a strong parenting role. But when children become adults, you hopefully learn to respect them as adults and build a relationship that mimics friendship in certain aspects of their lives. This question is for both of you. How was your experience completing these lists? How did it feel?"

Lydia answered first. "It was nice. It was actually somewhat of a relief. I got to see how even though they are grown up and away from home, I still am very much a part of their lives and they still need me. I was starting to feel unneeded, so this assignment was kind of a dose of reality."

"I agree," Martin said. "It showed me all that I've done for my children and the importance of my presence in their lives, even now."

I smiled at them and said, "That's great. Now, one thing that I noticed you all did not include was your roles as it relates to each other. So that will be tonight's homework. This time, don't bother writing two lists, just do one—the roles you play for your spouse."

I felt lighter the moment I finished mulling over the Woods' session. I was already in my PJs, so I dimmed the lights and climbed under the sheets. It was still early, but I was so sleep deprived that getting to bed early was a blessing.

Just as I was starting to doze off, the room's phone rang. I reached over and picked it up, thinking it was Lydia or Martin which were the only two people in the group who knew what room I was staying in.

"Hello?" I answered groggily.

The moment I heard the voice on the other end, my heart sank. It was Lem and he didn't sound happy at all.

Lesson 12: Peace Out

And your feet shod with the preparation of the gospel of peace.
(Ephesians 6:15)

Amber

The tension between Eric and I was so thick, you could have cut it with a knife. I knew he'd be somewhat hurt by my confession, but now that it was out in the open, he was more affected than I hoped. I understood that it had to be difficult to hear your wife tell you that she resents you and your child, but if I didn't get honest with myself, him, and Dr. Wilson, we might never get the healing we needed in our marriage.

The rest of the day dawdled by. Eric only spoke to me when necessary which conformed that he was offended. We went to lunch, walked down Washington and Collins, checking out the various stores, went swimming, hung out with Carl and Kelly for dinner, and watched movies in our room during the evening. I couldn't believe that I was on South Beach with my husband and we were spending so much time at odds with each other that we weren't enjoying all that Miami had to offer. I went to sleep praying that Tuesday would be a better day for us.

The next morning, I hopped out of bed enthusiastically, determined to shake Eric and I out of our marriage retreat funk. Eric still was in a sour mood, but I didn't let it deter me. During prayer, he tried not to hold my hand, and even had the audacity to pull away from me twice. That was when I had to set him straight.

"Listen, babe. I know that you aren't too happy about what I said yesterday in counseling, but if we are going to resolve our issues, we've got to tell the truth, even if it hurts the other person. I'm sorry for feeling the way I do. But I am here with you now, at this retreat, to figure out a way to overcome this whole sex thing and baby situation. Okay?"

Do you know that he looked at me and walked away? And I'm not talking about a few steps away. He left me standing there on the beach by myself!

I didn't like it, but I let him go. I ate breakfast with Carl and Kelly who actually seemed to be arguing less. Maybe this retreat was working for some of the couples, because at this point, I wasn't sure if it was helping me and Eric, or taking us to the point of no return.

I met Eric back at the hotel room thirty minutes before the couples' class. He still wasn't speaking much to me, so instead, we grabbed our beach chairs and headed over to the tent early. Lydia was teaching the class, and based on her track record, I felt confident that she would have some wisdom that would met both Eric and I right where we sat.

"We are now at the halfway point of our retreat," Lydia began. "It is Day Four and today we are going to provide you with another important piece of your spiritual armor—your shoes. You all know I can sometimes get excited and delay giving you the scripture, so let's take the time to read that now. Turn your Bibles to Ephesians 6:15."

She opened her Bible and flipped to the passage. "The Amplified version says, 'And having shod your feet in preparation—to face the enemy with firm-footed stability, the promptness and the readiness produced by the good news—of the Gospel of peace.' The scripture tells us that the next vital piece that we need to wear of the full armor of God are shoes that represent the Gospel of peace.

"Shoes? When there are people in this world that don't have or even wear shoes, why are shoes even necessary in God's armor?" she asked us rhetorically. "Couldn't God train us to be effective without shoes? Are they really that important?"

No one responded, but all eyes were focused on her, awaiting the answer. She placed her Bible down on her chair and said, "Well, some of the fastest runners that come out of third world nations learned to run without shoes. And if you're from a rural area, you know plenty of children that had to be forced to put on shoes because they spent half of their lives walking over rocks and all kinds of terrain without shoes. But shoes are still important. Our feet are not invincible, and even those people who are comfortable without shoes need to put on shoes from time to time when the weather or ground is not suitable to walk on barefoot. When it's cold outside and snowing, we need shoes to protect our feet so that we don't freeze to death from hypothermia. If we try to walk on sharp objects or surfaces like glass, we could get cut, or even if we step on extremely hot surfaces we can end up burned. Shoes provide a degree of protection for our feet in all of these situation. It is essential that our feet remain protected because without feet, it is extremely difficult to stand physically. Remember, we are putting all of this armor on so that we can *stand* spiritually against our enemy."

She slid her feet out of her flip flops and picked up the shoes, waving them in the air. She then put them back on the ground, slipped her feet back into them, and said, "So the Word tells us to put on these protective, spiritual shoes. The shoes are referred to as the Gospel of peace. Can you imagine being in the middle of a war, and there are gunshots everywhere, grenades blowing up in the distance, ashes surrounding you, screams of people who are hurt or scared? How much peace would you have in a situation like that? More than likely none. Your heart would be racing, you would be wondering if you're going to make it out alive or die, you might even panic and start crying or screaming yourself. But what if you were in that same situation and you felt at peace? Not peace because you like being in dangerous situations. But peace because you know that God is with you and will hide you under the shadow of His wings. Peace because you know that even in the middle of the battle, He is able to hide you in His secret place, He is able to make His angels encamp around you and keep you from even bumping your foot against a stone. If you were able to have that kind of peace in the midst of chaos, you'd be better equipped to strategize your next move, listen out for the enemy, and jump into action at the right time. In training for a war, you have to learn to remain calm and at peace so that your response is fight and not flight."

She held her right hand up in the air and made the universal peace symbol. "I think it was back in the 80's or 90's when there was this popular slang term 'peace out.' When someone was leaving from the presence of another, they would say, 'Peace out!' The term was another way to say goodbye, but if we really dissect it, we can receive it as a phrase of encouragement. It is almost as if the person is telling you to walk in peace or that they intend to walk in peace. I'm out in peace. I'm leaving in peace. You go out in peace. So for the rest of the day, when you see your spouse or another one of the couples in this retreat leaving, tell them, 'Peace out!' Encourage them to walk in peace. Pray for them to wear the shoes of the Gospel of peace. God's peace will protect you no matter where your feet take you. I'm going to take you all to church with this one, but look at your neighbor—which should be your spouse, and if he or she isn't, we might need to give you a double session with Dr. Wilson today!"

We all laughed.

"But for real, look at your neighbor and tell them, 'Peace out!'"

We all looked at our spouses, said, "Peace out!" and began to laugh. I glanced at Eric who seemed to soften up during the lesson. He still wasn't saying much to me, but he had managed to tell me "peace out" so I would take what I could get.

Once again, I was pleased with the message. I earnestly needed God's peace; it was just the thing that would help me let go of the grudge I had been carrying and enjoy the wonderful life I had with the man I loved.

As I watched Dr. Wilson leave the tent and walk back toward the hotel in preparation for our session, I gulped in anxiety, wondering what kind of emotional rollercoaster awaited us that day. Eric and I were already barely speaking. Was she right? Would it get even worse before it got better?

Lesson 13: A Time to Laugh

A time to weep and a time to laugh, a time to mourn and a time to dance (Ecclesiastes 3:4)

Blessed are you that hunger now: for you shall be filled. Blessed are you that weep now: for you shall laugh. (Luke 6:21)

Eric

I cannot begin to explain the thoughts and feelings that had overtaken me. Sitting in the previous day's counseling session, hearing Amber tell Dr. Wilson and I that she resented me and my child was too much to bear. I suspected that she had never gotten over the miscarriages and that they were a part of her sexual issues, and I even believed that deep down she blamed me. But to find out that her wounds extended to my daughter was distressing.

Amber had always treated Jonelle well, and she never once demonstrated to me that she had a problem with her being with us. But to think about it, I never asked. When we went to court about Jonelle, we were only fighting for joint custody. The judge threw us a curveball when he awarded primary custody to me. We never had the chance to discuss it, we just accepted the blessing and made room for Jonelle in our home.

I guess I never asked Amber how she felt because I didn't want her to feel anything but happy about my daughter being in our home. I knew that Amber loved Jonelle, but I rarely considered what having my child always around was like for her, especially when Amber kept losing her own babies. Yet, it still infuriated me that she could be angry and even jealous of a little girl who didn't choose any of this. I thought Amber was better than that.

They say you never fully get to know a person. They say that even after many years of marriage, you still find yourself learning new things about your spouse. I now believed it. Seeing this side of Amber that held a grudge against those who loved her over something that none of us could control was disheartening. It made me sick to my stomach, and I spent the rest of that day emotionally disconnected from her.

On Tuesday morning, she tried to act like Monday never happened. I knew Monday was real because I had tossed and turned in my sleep all night long dreaming about our counseling session. During sunrise prayer, she did "an Amber" and tried to read me my rights when I didn't want to hold her hand. Usually, I would have just let Amber have her way, but that morning, I couldn't have cared less about what Amber wanted. I let her speak her mind, then I responded by leaving her to pray by herself. I was certain that she didn't expect that outcome.

I skipped breakfast and watched TV instead. I just wasn't hungry. In the middle of the couples' class, I regretted that decision when my stomach started to growl, but what could I do about it then? I would have to wait until lunch to nourish myself. It was a good thing that the lesson was an interesting one, and I forgot about my hunger as I ate the spiritual food Lydia gave us on walking in peace. By the time the lesson had ended, I felt a rise in my spirit. I still wasn't happy with Amber's remarks, but I was willing to let the peace of God which surpasses all understanding guard my heart and my mind.

"So I imagine that you two didn't have the best day yesterday," Dr. Wilson said at the beginning of our therapy session.

I glanced over at Amber who was looking back and forth between me and Dr. Wilson. When I didn't speak up, she replied, "No, not really. How did you know?"

Dr. Wilson sighed and said, "It's written all over your faces. Your body language demonstrates a disconnection from each other, more so today than the previous days. Plus, you said some very powerful words yesterday. The truth, but powerful."

"So what do we do now?" Amber asked.

"Well, that's up to you two," Dr. Wilson responded. "I can tell that Eric is the one that holds the relationship together."

Amber gasped. "Excuse me?"

"Most times in marriages, there is someone who keeps the relationship going no matter what. It's not about who loves whom more or anything like that. It's merely about who wants or needs the relationship most. From watching the two of you together, it appears that Eric is the one that keeps the two of you going, sort of like he's the glue."

"So are you saying that I'm not committed to my marriage?" Amber said, seeming slighted.

Dr. Wilson shook her head. "No, I'm not saying that. What I'm saying is that probably, in most cases, he is the one that fights for the relationship more than you. When you get into disagreements, he's probably the one who gives in first or tries to resolve the issue. The peacekeeper. Am I wrong?"

She really had us all figured out. I was impressed. "You're actually dead on," I said. "I'm the one who usually makes the most compromises. It's not that Amber doesn't go to bat for us, but I do it more often."

"I don't want you two to think this is a bad thing. It just is what it is," Dr. Wilson stated. "In relationships, everyone plays their roles. Relationships are balanced when both people play complementary parts, not the same role. This is not only the case for marriages, but any kind of relationship—parent-child bonds, friendships, and so on. Each person has something unique to give. I bring this up in counseling because since Eric is the glue, if he stops trying, it puts your relationship in a state of crisis. Amber will either have to take on his role and become the glue until Eric is ready to play his part again, or the relationship will fall apart. The problem is then whether Amber can adjust to being the new glue. Sometimes we are so comfortable with our roles that taking on a new position is too much change."

"Okay, I'm confused," Amber replied.

"What I am saying, Amber, is that you're going to have to be more proactive about making this marriage work. Yes, you've been through a lot, and yes, you've probably been a really good wife, but it's time for you to really show Eric how badly you want this marriage. On the flipside, Eric, your wife is hurting and you are going to have to be more aware of her needs. If she is telling you that she's in pain, it doesn't mean that she should just get over it, it means that she wants you to help her get through whatever she is going through. Both of you are going to have to do the work. It's not going to happen on its own."

"Okay," Amber said. "I'm willing to do my part. I just don't know where to start."

"Me neither," I said.

Dr. Wilson grinned. "The two Fs. Forgiveness and Fun."

"What?" I asked.

"You're on SoBe walking around like your puppy just died. You both need to go out and have some fun—together. Not only that, but both of you will have to forgive each other and maybe even yourselves for whatever pain you've afflicted upon the other person."

Amber huffed. "Why does it seem like all we ever do is forgive each other?"

"Because that's marriage, sweetie," Dr. Wilson replied. "It's a constant cycle of forgiveness. No matter how great your marriage is, eventually someone is going to do something that requires forgiveness. The quicker you both learn how to keep forgiving each other, the smoother your relationship will run. But the day you two stop being willing to forgive each other, is the day your marriage is doomed. Trust me on that one."

I scratched my head. "Dr. Wilson, what's SoBe?"

She looked at me as if I had lost my mind. "South Beach. You two really need to get out more."

"Oh." Maybe she had a point.

"One more thing," Dr. Wilson said. "Understand this. Forgiveness is more than just saying that you forgive someone. You have to let it go which means to a certain extent you have to forget about it. You know the saying, forgive and forget? Well despite popular opinion, it's true. When God forgives us, He separates our sins from us and remembers them no more. Now, I'm not telling you that you all of a sudden get a case of amnesia, but you have to get to a point where whatever wrong was done against you doesn't matter anymore. That's how you forget. Until you get to the point where it doesn't matter, the wrong will be replayed over and over again in your mind, and the moment another wrong is committed, that previous wrong will be thrown back out into the open. To truly forgive someone, you must cast out the offense by saying and believing that it doesn't matter anymore. Forgive the person and forget about the offense so that you can truly move past it."

We took Dr. Wilson up on her advice and decided to let our hair down in Miami a smidge. Amber, trying to play the role of the "glue"—whatever that was—got us tickets at the Improv in Coconut Grove, another neighborhood in Miami about a fifteen minute drive from SoBe—I was hip to the lingo now. Since it was a Tuesday night, the Improv had a line-up called Traditional

Tuesdays where they brought in various mid-level comedians. In addition, Coconut Grove had a movie theater, so we also got tickets to catch the most recent action flick staring Dwayne Johnson also known as The Rock.

The comedy show was awesome. Although we had an Improv Comedy Club in Atlanta, Amber and I were so busy trying to run our businesses that we rarely took out the time to do fun activities. Our idea of hanging out was renting a movie, ordering pizza, and lounging around the house. When Amber needed to release tension, she called her best friend and they went out shopping or to the spa. When I needed a break, I went out to shoot some hoops, played pool, or watched a sports game with the fellas. With the exception of going out to a nice restaurant or attending church together, Amber and I rarely ventured into public together for down-time events. I figured our behavior was pretty typical of married couples because most of the married men I knew were the same way. Maybe we'd become too comfortable in our relationships and had forgotten how to make time for the enjoyable aspects of married life. Maybe this was one of the areas where Dr. Wilson was trying to get me to pay more attention.

Leave it to Amber, we had prime seating, up close near the stage. The moment the waitress led us to our seats, I knew that we were in trouble.

"Amber," I muttered in a low voice. "Why are we sitting in the front?"

She glared at me as if I had just asked her the square root of 1,784. "Because I want to see. I don't want to sit in the back. Isn't segregation over? Why colored folks always want to sit in the back still?"

I almost laughed at her question because for some crazy reason, it was true. "Babe," I said instead. "You don't want to sit in the front of a comedy club. The comedians will crack jokes about us. We need to go to the back."

"If you want to go sit in the back where you can't see, be my guest. But I'm not moving. And if these comedians don't have any better jokes than to talk about me, they aren't that funny to begin with."

She had a point. I was nervous, but I wasn't going to leave Amber in the front by herself. We were supposed to be spending the evening together having fun. I just hoped my ego could handle anything the comedians could dish out.

To my relief, the jokes about the people in the front of the room weren't too bad. Of course, the comedians took out the time to search for a few vulnerable attendees they could laugh at, but thank God they left me and Amber alone for the most part. There was a guy with a mouth full of gold teeth sitting a couple of rows back who bore the brunt of any impromptu jests. The only time Amber and I were in the spotlight was when one of the comedians thought it would be funny to try to hit on Amber. I knew the whole routine of male comics finding a pretty woman and flattering her while at the same time trying to keep her man from getting too jealous. I brushed his advances away as entertainment, and winked at Amber who was slightly embarrassed, whispering to her, "I told you we should have sat in the back."

When the comedy show was over, we went straight to the theater. Our movie was scheduled to start about thirty minutes after the comedy show, so we picked a seat in the middle of the theater and talked about the Improv comedians until the movie began.

I loved watching action movies with Amber because she couldn't handle the suspense. She jumped and ducked every time someone started shooting and constantly asked, "What's gonna happen next?" Her heart rate was speeding the entire film. And when the movie reached its climax, she shoved her face into my chest, afraid to completely watch the ending, but peeking out here and there to avoid missing the details.

We caught a cab back to SoBe after the film. It was around midnight by the time we reached our hotel which in South Beach meant party time. Still buzzing with energy, we decided to walk down Ocean and check out the nightlife. The weather was perfect, a mild 75 degrees with a light breeze that came in from the sea. We approached a club that played Latino music like Salsa and Meringue. There was a ten dollar cover charge to get in, but the manager at the front door begged us so much to go inside that he let us in for free.

The inside of the club was dimly lit yet decorated in floral colors and designs. The place wasn't packed, but there were enough patrons to make it appear like a happening spot. In South Beach, midnight was still considered early, so I suspected that more people would encroach upon the club as time passed.

Amber wanted to dance, but I didn't know anything about Salsa dancing and I wasn't going to get caught looking silly. The people in the club were dancing like they just left a taping of *Dancing with the Stars*. With my luck, I would have tripped over my own feet and ended up spending the rest of the retreat on crutches. I told Amber to go dance as I took a seat against the wall.

A man who looked like a bootleg Ricky Martin saw Amber alone and asked her to dance. She immediately peered over at me to see if I would be offended if she took him up on his offer. Although I didn't like to see anyone touching my lady, I also didn't want to ruin her night with my envy, so I nodded in agreement. Amber and the fake Ricky dance for eight songs. I know it was eight songs because I counted. Eight long Spanish songs with someone yelling out lyrics that I could not even attempt to translate into English.

At the end of song number eight, I stood up to inform Amber that it was time to leave. She bowed out of the ninth song and fake Ricky kissed her on the back of her hand before she could walk away. For a moment I saw a news headline flash in front of my eyes.

HUSBAND ATTACKS FAKE RICKY MARTIN IN SOBE. MAN IN CRITICAL CONDITION.

I shook off the idea when Amber grabbed my hand and led me out of the club. Thank God for always providing a way out of temptation.

Lesson 14: A Time to Harvest

A time to be born and a time to die. A time to plant and a time to harvest. (Ecclesiastes 3:2)

Let both grow together until the harvest: and in the time of harvest I will say to the reapers, Gather ye together first the tares, and bind them in bundles to burn them: but gather the wheat into my barn. (Matthew 13:30)

Dr. Wilson

I knew that my husband loved me, but I hadn't expected his phone call. I had never in all of our years of marriage seen him as angry as he was when he walked out the night prior. Lem was like a quiet storm. He wasn't aggressive or forceful, but when he had enough, you did not want to be on the receiving side of his wrath. He had told me stories about how people had pushed him over the edge in the past and his fury-like response. Yet, I had always played my cards right with him and therefore had never witnessed firsthand him reaching the end of his rope.

Although he didn't do much or even say much when he left, him leaving spoke volumes. I was wondering if the next time I saw his face would be in divorce court. My imagination had even taken me back home to find a house empty of Lem and all of his possessions—which were really my possessions too. So when I heard his ill-tempered voice on the other end of the phone, I was shocked and a tad scared.

"Lem," I said, unsure of what he might say next.

"What?" His 'what' sounded like a response he would give to a pestering child, not his wife of five years.

"Are you okay?" It was the best reply I could come up with considering the circumstances.

"Andrea, are you serious? What do you think?"

"Probably not. So . . . why did you call?" It might have been a bad question to ask, but the tension was killing me and he wasn't being forthcoming. If he was going to tell me he wanted a divorce, I wanted him to just say it and get it over with. Don't take all day.

He got quiet which frightened me even more. Lem wasn't a man of many words, but what he said, he meant. He was a thinker, and even through the phone I could sense his mind moving.

"I gotta go," he mumbled and hung up the phone. My body froze. I could hear the phone disconnect and even the dial tone, but I didn't automatically place the receiver back down on the hook. This was bad. He couldn't even say what he wanted to say. Because he called the room phone, there was no caller ID and I had no idea where he was calling me from. He could have been back in New York by now or somewhere else, who knew?

I heard the phone start to ring in my hand, indicating that I had held it off the hook to long and the annoying beeps would begin soon. I finally hung it up and picked up my cellular from off the nightstand. I needed to know where he was and what his phone call meant. How could I actively and fully participate in the next day's counseling sessions if the fate of my marriage was inconclusive? I speed dialed his cell phone. The voicemail picked up instantly letting me know that either his phone was dead or turned off. Frantically, I dialed our home phone, but after the four standard rings, the voicemail picked up there too.

"You've just reached the Wilson household," I heard my own voice say in a cheerful tone. "No one is available to take your call, but if you leave a message after the tone, we'll get back to you as soon as we can. Thanks and have a blessed day." Beep.

"L-Lem, this is Andrea," I stuttered. "If you're there, pick up." I waited a few moments, hoping I would hear his voice again. I didn't. "Okay, well call me when you get this message. We really need to talk."

I pressed END on my phone to disconnect the call. I sat there stunned, unsure of what to do next. I thought about my voice on the voicemail greeting. What if this was the beginning of the end of the Wilson household? What if my next greeting went back to Joyner, my maiden name? Nope. Whether we lasted or not, I was keeping Wilson. I had achieved too much under his last name. I would be like Tina Turner. I would fight to keep my name.

Really, Andrea? I couldn't believe that my husband was who knows where, and I was mentally debating about whether or not I would go back to my maiden name. I was a marriage counselor for heaven's sake! I needed to fight for my marriage and not over a name. What was wrong with me?

I tossed my cell phone back onto the nightstand and pulled the bed sheets back on top of me. Martin and Lydia were teaching the group how to fight for our marriages, and I needed to start paying more attention. Based on Lem's dismal sounding voice, I was in for the fight of my life.

Tuesday morning, I woke up with a renewed sense of urgency. My plan was to get all that I could get out of the remainder of the retreat, to help my clients to value and grow in their marriages, and to get back home to save my own. I went to sunrise prayer alone again with my head held high as if it were all good in my world. There was no need to alarm the rest of the group because I was in a crisis. In my personal prayer area, I apologized to God about being hard-headed the day before. I didn't want to gain everything at the cost of losing the most precious parts of my life. I had become a psychologist that specialized in marriage therapy because I loved marriage and all that it represented. I hated seeing people broken from the sting of divorce. My heart desired to stand up to the tricks and tactics of the devil, and to help others to find a way back to love.

I prayed that God would give me the right attitude to help the couples on the retreat as I had been paid to do. "Lord help me not to get so wrapped up in my own problems that I forget to be the light that You called me to be. Each of these couples need something that only You can provide. Help me to lead them back into Your presence where there is liberty, redemption, and restoration."

I also prayed that God would show me how to bring Lem and I back to a place of oneness. We were operating as two separate individuals instead of one flesh as God made us to be when we married. "Father, we've both made mistakes. He operated without me and I withheld from him. That is not how two people who are supposed to be one flesh should conduct themselves. Teach us how to truly be one. Show us how to reject individuality and to walk in harmony as a team."

I emerged from prayer feeling serene. I know that it was divine confirmation when Lydia's couple's class was on wearing the shoes of peace. God's message to me was clear—don't allow the enemy or anyone else to steal our peace. Having a peaceful mindset would help me and Lem to make the right decisions in our marriage. It was when we lost our peace that we made a mess. His lack of peace over having the funds to pay his employees led to him making a desperate choice to pay them with our money without consulting with me. My lack of peace over him spending our bill money without conferring with me led me to use harsh words against him in an attempt to punish him for his mistakes.

Both of us were guilty of not walking in peace. Both of us would have to learn to put on God's full armor daily.

After my counseling sessions for the day, I returned to the beach to debrief as I'd done the majority of the retreat. Today was a much better day for all of the sessions, and I knew that my willingness to let God use me regardless of my marital woes had positively impacted my ability to assist the couples in the group. I closed my eyes and remembered each session.

Eric and Amber. I knew that the night prior would be a cold night in the Hayes suite. They walked into my office looking defeated. I honestly felt bad for them. I'm certain that if Lem and I were going to marriage therapy we would have probably worn the same expressions on our faces as Eric and Amber.

They needed to have fun. Amber was so much like me that it was scary. She was smart and focused which were good traits most times, but more than likely, every once in a while these characteristics were to her detriment. I used to be like her, taking life a little too seriously. But dating and marrying Lem had loosened me up, and now I knew how to relax. Amber had not learned that lesson yet, and Eric was so busy trying to figure out who he was and how he had won such a great wife that he didn't know how to relax either. So I gave them an assignment. Go out and have fun. Explore Miami. Go dance, laugh, eat like it's your last meal, party until the lights come on in the club. Okay, well, I didn't tell them that last suggestion. It was a Christian marriage retreat after all and they had sunrise prayer that they needed to attend.

They both stared at me as if I had lost my mind when I recommended they go out. I guess they were expecting one of my more structured assignments like writing a list. Some couples like Carl and Kelly needed more structure because they were already out of control and needed to be reeled in, while other like the

Hayes clan needed less structure because they were so tightly wound that they might crack if you touched them. They needed to get a life.

And speaking of Carl and Kelly . . .

Carl and Kelly. I was glad to see Carl and Kelly walk into counseling not at each other's throats. They still wouldn't win any prizes for the Couple of the Year, but it was an improvement. I also couldn't believe they actually completed their homework. Kelly must have come home early from the club last night. All jokes aside, I was pleased with them.

Kelly was the first to share her list of outlets and stressors. "As an outlet, I go shopping, to the bar or a party, to the movies, to the gym, to the beach or on vacation, to plays, and hang out over my friends' houses. The responsibilities that stress me out most are having to take the girls everywhere they need to go, having to keep the house clean when no one else is helping out, and having to be the one to stay on top of the girls' schoolwork."

"Kelly, when it comes to raising your daughters and taking care of the home, how much do you feel that Carl helps out?" I asked.

"Hardly ever," Kelly answered.

I nodded, taking it all in. "Give me a percentage. What's your percentage versus his?"

"I probably do like 80-90 percent while he does 10-20 percent."

"Carl, is this true?"

Carl sighed. "I think she's over-exaggerating a little. Yes, she does a lot more than me at home and with the girls, but I think I do more than 10 or 20 percent."

Kelly rolled her eyes. "No, you don't. I do everything at home."

"Carl, I think what your wife is trying to tell you is that she needs more help around the house and with the girls. Quite possibly, the reason she's rebelling against home life is because it's become too much. By her working two jobs and going out frequently now, she's forcing you to step up and help out more often."

"I never thought about it like that, but I guess you have a point," Kelly said. "I wasn't purposely trying to abandon my family, but I just felt like I needed an escape."

"I mean, if I need to help out more to relieve some of the burden on her, I can do that. I just don't want her escaping out to the club every weekend," Carl said.

"Carl, what's on your lists?" I asked.

"Okay, I've got working out, playing basketball, watching football, going to church, fishing, playing cards, and going to a concert as my outlets. The only responsibility that stresses me out is making sure I make enough money to pay the bills. I'm a real estate agent so I get paid off commissions. Sometimes when the market is slow, I worry about whether I'll bring in enough income to cover our expenses."

"So how do you feel when you are worried about money and Kelly uses her extra cash from her second job to buy expensive purses and clothes?" I asked.

Carl scratched his head. "I like for her to have nice things, so I don't have a problem with her buying a purse or whatnot. But sometimes I wish she would say, 'I have some extra money. Do you need me to help you with anything?' Also, sometimes I want to buy her the nice things she wants, but either it's too expensive at the time or she doesn't give me a chance to do it for her before she goes out and does it for herself."

"What I am hearing is that there is a lack of communication between the two of you," I said. "Carl, Kelly wants you to help out more around the house and give her a break with the girls. Kelly, Carl wants you to help him sometimes financially and allow him to spoil you. I think if both of you can find a way to express yourself with your words and not your actions, and if both of you are willing to make some minor changes, you two could have a healthier marriage."

They gazed at me in awe as if I just solved all of their problem in a blink. I hadn't. There was difference between identifying the issue and working on the solution.

"Okay, your next assignment is this—I want you to take your list of stressors and together work out a plan of what each of you are willing to do to alleviate some of the stress of the other person. And be specific. Don't just say, I'm going to help out more or I'll give him some money. Write down the details. For instance, I will take the girls to soccer practice on Tuesdays and Thursdays or I will check in with him twice a month to see if there are any outstanding bills that need to be paid. This assignment is about learning to compromise for the sake of the marriage. Understand?"

They agreed. Finally.

Franklin and Tamela. I tried to engage the Days in another conversation about preparing to die, but they wouldn't allow it. Instead, Tamela busted me out and asked, "Sweetheart, where's your husband?"

"Uh, what?" I asked, feeling completely caught off guard.

She gave me a feisty smirk and said, "I asked you, where is your husband?"

Awe man! I was trapped. I couldn't lie to the pastor and his wife. They were both looking at me as if they were demanding to know. I had to come clean. So much for my perfect psychologist façade. "He's . . . he's not here."

She gave me an unimpressed look. "We know that already. Where is he?"

I shrugged. "Ma'am, the truth is I don't know."

She slapped her thigh and Franklin laughed. "You don't know?" Tamela asked. "Why don't you know where your husband is? He's not a sock or an earring that you just somehow lose. Explain to us how you lost your husband."

I sighed. "It's a long story. Really."

She down looked at her watch. "We've got time. A whole fifty minutes to be exact."

I glared at them to nonverbally communicate that I didn't want to talk about it, but they weren't budging.

"We're waiting," Tamela said in a scolding tone.

I took a deep breath and told them the story, starting from me throwing away Lem's swimming trunk and finding out our account was overdrawn to him calling me last night and hanging up. By the time I finished the story, I was in tears.

"I'm sorry for crying," I said. "And I'm supposed to be the therapist."

Tamela passed me the box of Kleenex that until this point had been purposed for my clients, not me. "It's okay, dear. I asked you what happened and you told me. There's nothing wrong with a few tears shed over a sad story."

Franklin intervened. "We just wanted to give you a chance to talk about what you're going through. We noticed that he hasn't been with you lately and you've looked a little sad. We understand that it's hard for you to feel comfortable leaning on us when you're here to be a part of the support system for us, but the great thing about the body of Christ is that we are all here to lean on each other. At least, that's the way it's supposed to be."

"Thanks," I said with a sniffle.

"So, sweetheart," Tamela said. "Do you think you did the right thing?"

"I know I did the wrong thing. The worst part is that as I was single-handedly ruining my marriage, I knew I was making a mistake. I don't know—it just felt good to say the wrong thing. It might sound crazy, but for someone like me who always does what's right, it was nice to just be destructive."

"I'm going to offer you two perspectives," Franklin said. "The obvious one is what we've been discussing in the couples' class all week—spiritual warfare. The enemy wants to break down your family, all of our families. But especially yours because you are in the marriage ministry. If the enemy can get you to break up your marriage and stop believing in this union, you will no longer be in a position to help others the way you've been doing all week long."

I nodded. "That makes sense."

"The second perspective isn't so obvious, but it's one that my wife and I know all too well. When you're in an elevated position, a position of leadership like we are—and I am including you when I say we—there is a pressure to be an example which means people never expect you to fail. No one wants to fail, but failure is a part of life and success. When people don't give you permission to fail, it can be like a prison. You are a prisoner of your own success. You have to constantly be perfect because if you aren't, everyone will watch you fall and judge you as being a fake. It's a huge burden to bear, and sometimes when someone like us gets tired of carrying that weight, we purposely sabotage our own success, just to get a break, just to be free from the prison of success. Sound familiar?"

"Oh wow. Yes. Too familiar. That's exactly how I feel."

"We've been there, done that, and bought the t-shirt," Tamela said.

"So how did you all handle feeling that way?"

"We stopped pretending with those around us. You are the only one causing people to believe that you're perfect. Once you strip yourself of the façade and start being real with others about your flaws, no one will expect so much from you," Franklin said.

"We just tell people the truth about who we are before they make us in their minds who they want us to be," Tamela added.

"You will have to learn to define yourself, for yourself," said Franklin. "Stop letting other people decide who you are. There are only two in this world who can truly make that decision—you and God."

My session with the Days ended with me being counseled instead of them. Go figure.

Jordan and Sarah. I continued to work with the Larks on Couples Communication. I reviewed the day prior's lesson on communicating sensory data, thoughts and feelings, then introduced them to the next step on The Awareness Wheel, expressing wants.

"There are three parts to the want section," I told them. "Wants for self, wants for others, and wants for us. You want to address each subsection of wants when communicating with your partner. Going back to the original example of wanting to go out to dinner, Sarah might say, 'I want for myself to be able to have a break from cooking. I want for myself to feel loved and appreciated by experiencing romantic dinners away from home. I want for you, Jordan, to get out of the house more often for social activities. I want for you to treat me to dinner. I want for us to bring the romance back into our lives. I want for us to have fun together again.' Did you both follow how I communicated wants for self, others, and us?"

They both said yes. I was glad that they were speaking more. Maybe the prior lesson had opened them up. I allowed them to return back to their selected issue of Jordan withdrawing and to communicate to each other their wants. Once they had done so adequately, I had them select another issue and to use it to express their perspective starting with sensory data and going through wants. Jordan got to pick the problem this time and he chose Sarah's tendency to coddle their son. I was proud of their progress, and told them that on Wednesday, we would cover the final section of The Awareness Wheel—actions.

Martin and Lydia. The Woods, once again, came to their session ready with their completed lists of spousal roles.

Martin share his list first. "I see myself as a protector, provider, leader, supporter, affection giver, comforter, and spiritual head."

"What about you Lydia?" I asked after we dissected Martin's list.

"Okay, I am a preparer, helpmeet, encourager, prayer warrior, nurturer, giver of affection, and motivator."

We reviewed her roles for a few minutes before I said, "I had you both write these lists so that you can physically see all that has not changed since your children left home. Sometimes we get so caught up in what we think we have lost, that we don't consider what we still have that is just as important. The both of you are in a new season of your lives. You two have such an awesome ministry with each other, but also with the world. Just like this retreat, you are helping others to learn God's word and to be more successful in their lives. When your children were still in the home, what you could do for others was limited because you had to physically be there to meet your children's needs. But now that your kids have left the nest, you are freed up to be all that God has called you to become."

I looked at both of them and said, "You all might hate me, but I have to ask you to do one last homework assignment. This time, I want you to create one list together. This list is what roles you play for God and His Kingdom. Don't do it separately, do it together as a couple. I want to see one list on one sheet of paper that represents both of your spiritual roles."

Waves crashing against the shoreline was the first sound I heard when I came out of my daze. I opened my eyes slowly and took in the various sights of the beach—children playing, women working on their suntans, guys playing Frisbee and beach volleyball. I felt good. I still didn't know where my husband was, but I knew that God would take care of Him, and hopefully lead him back to me in due time.

I got up and took a walk down the strip, deciding to enjoy dinner for one at an Italian restaurant. As I ate, I people watched. I liked to observe others when no one knew they were being watched, seeing them authentically. I think that was where I first learned my love for behavioral science, when I realized that I wanted to know what made people tick. I monitored a few random couples, guessing whether they were married or dating, and their level of satisfaction in the relationship. I would never know if I was right or not, but the answer didn't matter. I just enjoyed the process.

I wish I could say I felt the same way about my marriage—that the process mattered more than having answers, but that wasn't true.

That evening, I once again lay in bed alone, thinking about Lem. I had grown so accustomed to sleeping with him by my side that not having him there for multiple nights in a row was depressing. I turned on the flat screen TV and watched a few crime documentaries. If Lem were with me, those were the kind of shows he would have been watching. I really missed him.

Just as I was turning the TV off to get some sleep, my room's phone rang out, I instantly suspected it was Lem and dove across the bed to answer it.

"Hello! Lem?" I answered. I immediately felt stupid because I realized that if it wasn't him, but was someone like Lydia, I would have blown my cover.

"Yeah," he replied, causing me instant relief.

"Where are you? Are you home?" I asked rapidly.

"I just wanted to check on you," he said, ignoring my questions. I knew my husband well enough to take the hint. If I asked him a question and he didn't respond to it right away, he

A'ndrea J. Wilson

didn't want me to know the answer. I really wanted to know his location, but I was picking my battles wisely so I chose to let it go.

He said he wanted to check on me which meant that he hadn't given up on us yet. It was Lem-code to say he still cared. "Thanks," I replied. "I appreciate your concern. I'm okay. What about you? Are you okay?"

"I'm alright. Like I said, I just wanted to check on you."

He was talking in circles. More than likely, he wanted to say more, but hadn't found the courage to say what was really on his mind. So I attempted to help him. "I miss you," I said.

"You do?" he asked.

"Yeah, I do."

"Um, well, I have to go, so I'll talk to you later. Bye, Andrea."

"Goodbye, Lem."

I hung up the phone feeling confused. On one hand, he'd called and said that he wanted to check on me. That was excellent news because it meant that he was thinking about me and he wanted me to know that I mattered to him. Yet, on the other hand, when I opened up and told him that I missed him, he didn't return the sentiment. I had to admit that it hurt my feelings to not hear him say the words back to me. Did he not miss me? Did he care, but not enough to want me back? And where was he anyways? I had tried to call the house phone again earlier in the day and he hadn't picked up so I wasn't sure if he was back in Rochester. Could he have made a detour to another city? Was he at home, watching the house phone ring, but just letting me sweat it out?

I huffed at the endless string of questions filling my mind. Before he called, I was ready to drift off to sleep, but after having the brief conversation with him, I was wide awake. I wondered how long it would take me to push the dozens of questions that I couldn't answer out of my mind enough to fall asleep. That night I found out that it took two and a half hours. Bah humbug!

Lesson 15: 'Tis So Sweet

Above all, taking the shield of faith, where with ye shall be able
to quench all of the fiery darts of the wicked.
(Ephesians 6:16)

Eric

The next morning after my evening out with my wife I felt
optimistic. I could tell that Amber was in a good mood as
well. We practically leaped out of bed that morning and skipped
down to sunrise prayer. Our one-on-one prayer time on the beach
seemed unusually intimate, and it took everything in me to keep
my mind focused on the prayer and not on how beautiful my wife
looked as the sun crept up in the horizon.

We ate breakfast with Carl and Kelly who surprisingly
weren't arguing. Kelly actually was fully dressed and didn't look
hung-over from the night before. Could this retreat really be
bringing out the best in all of us?

I was excited about getting to the couples' class. We only had
three days left of the retreat and I'd come to cherish the inspiring
messages provided daily by the Woods. Lydia led Wednesday's
class and Amber appeared happy to see her mentor teaching
again.

"Good morning again, everyone," Lydia greeted us. "Day
Five is probably one of the most important lessons. Not that all of

the armor of God isn't highly essential, but this item separates the haves from the have nots. Follow me to Ephesians 6:16 to see what I'm talking about."

We all turned to the scripture in our Bibles and followed along. "The Word says, 'Lift up over all the—covering—shield of saving faith, upon which you can quench all of the flaming missiles of the wicked one.' That's the Amplified Version, but the King James Version starts off saying, 'Above all, take the shield of faith.' So we can gather from this verse that our next spiritual piece of armor is a shield that represents faith," she said.

"What is faith? The Word tells us that faith is the substance of things hoped for and the evidence of things not seen. It means that the beginning of faith is believing and trusting what you don't have or can't see, and that the end of faith is obtaining that thing because of your belief. Faith allows you to receive what you don't have. We did not have salvation, but the moment we believed and confessed that Jesus is Lord, our faith ushered in God's gift of eternal life."

She made eye contact with all of us before continuing. "There is a term for when someone believes something negative about themselves, and that belief results in bad circumstances for the person. It's called a self-fulfilling prophecy. This theory suggests that if I believe negativity about myself, my life will reflect my beliefs. Of course, the opposite is true. If I believe positivity about myself, my life will reflect my beliefs as well."

I nodded my head, understanding what she was talking about. A few others grunted in agreement.

"The opposite of faith is doubt," Lydia said. "The biggest weapon the enemy uses against us is doubt. If evil can get you to doubt yourself, and even more so God, you can't win, you can't stand. The fiery darts are doubt. It is those thoughts and feelings that tell you that you can't do it, God is not real or He's not with you. How can you fight and win if you don't believe you stand a chance? Therefore having faith is imperative to the battle. When the verse says 'above all' in the King James Version, it's saying that if you don't have anything else to protect yourself with, hold up that shield of faith. When the verse says 'lift up over' in the Amplified, it's saying raise above all of your other gear the shield of faith. Either way you want to slice it, that shield of faith has the ability to protect you in ways that are essential to your survival."

"Amen," Pastor Franklin yelled out.

Lydia smiled and continued. "For example, when you are ready to give up on the marriage, and you don't have any peace, you can't decipher what's the truth, you don't even feel saved or in right standing with God anymore, faith can keep you. By believing and trusting that God is able to do exceedingly abundantly above all that you can imagine, and believing that you can do all things through Christ who gives you strength, you can stand in that marriage, you can go another day or week or year until the storm ceases and God delivers you. Doubt is what crushes your dreams and leaves you feeling hopeless and helpless. Faith is what rescues you and gives you victory over everything, including the grave."

By this point, we were getting excited about her lesson and more of us responded verbally with words like "Amen" and "Yes."

Lydia slowed down the message and said, "A song came to my heart as I was preparing for this lesson, the hymn, 'Tis So Sweet.' I love the way the lyrics remind me of the beauty of believing God at His Word. My thoughts about the song led me to look it up online, and I found out there is a very remarkable story behind the song. The songwriter is a woman named Louisa M. R. Stead who lived in the 1800's and died in 1917. When she was twenty-five, she married and had a daughter. Several years later, she watched her husband drown as he attempted to save the life of a child who also drowned. In her bereavement, she wrote the lyrics to 'Tis So Sweet.' She did go on to become a missionary and to marry again. I always find it so amazing that some of the most memorable songs are created in the midst of a storm. It's easy to believe in God and to praise Him when life is calm, but when the winds blow and the rain comes, these are the moments that reveal to us the authenticity of our faith in God.

"I want us to end our lesson today by singing the hymn 'Tis So Sweet.' As you sing along, consider that these word were not written by someone in the happiest season of their life, but someone who had just lost her spouse and could have easily turned her back on God. Instead of blaming God, she raised up her shield of faith and believed that His Word was true. Let us sing."

> *'Tis so sweet to trust in Jesus,*
> *And to take Him at His Word;*
> *Just to rest upon His promise,*
> *And to know, 'Thus says the Lord!'*
> *Jesus, Jesus, how I trust Him!*
> *How I've proved Him o'er and o'er*
> *Jesus, Jesus, precious Jesus!*
> *O for grace to trust Him more!*

By the time we all finished singing the hymn, there was not a dry eye inside that tent.

Lesson 16: A Time to Mourn

A time to weep and a time to laugh; a time to mourn and a time to dance. (Ecclesiastes 2:4)

Blessed are they that mourn: for they shall be comforted. (Matthew 5:4)

Amber

I was moved by the couples' class on Wednesday about faith. I had been complaining about losing my unborn children, but I had not considered all of the people that I had not lost. Hearing the story of the hymnist who tragically lost her husband in front of her eyes, but went on to trust and praise God anyway, instantly convicted me. I was guilty of being unfaithful to God. The moment life didn't go my way, I blamed Him and turned my back on Him.

By the time I entered the counseling suite, I was seconds away from tears. It seemed the entire retreat I'd been crying which was really unlike me. I knew I wasn't pregnant, but my hormones felt like they were on steroids. Yet, it wasn't a drug that had me emotional, it was the healing process that I had to go through if I ever wanted to have a normal life again.

"Amber?" Dr. Wilson said to me the moment she saw my watery eyes. "What's going on?"

I peeped at Eric who appear just as concerned and ignorant about my brink of tears. I opened my mouth to explain, but instead of words, an uncontained wail spilled out of my mouth.

No one stopped me from crying, they just let me rip. Dr. Wilson and Eric traded places, him sitting in her usual chair and she positioned next to me on the sofa. She began to rub my back like my mother used to do when I was a little girl. The comforting sensation of her touch sent my bawling into a frenzy. I hadn't cried that hard since . . . my first miscarriage. The thought of it gave me another reason to cry, prolonging my episode.

Fifteen minutes later, I was all cried out. I had used half a box of tissues and I was sure my face looked like a big, red, swollen tomato. "I'm-I'm sorry," I sniffled, looking up to see two sets of eyes watching me closely.

Dr. Wilson stopped consoling me and said, "Do you want to tell us what that was about?"

I took a few deep breaths before speaking. I wasn't sure if I would start crying again or be able to speak this time.

"It . . . the . . . ," I said, trying to contain my emotions.

"Take your time," Dr. Wilson said, sounding like one of those old church mothers during testimony service. Thinking about church mothers caused me to giggle which made it a little easier to talk.

"The class today was powerful," I said. "That lady's story, the one who wrote the song was . . . it made me think about all that I have instead of what I don't have. She lost her husband. I still have mine. But even after losing him, she trusted God and wrote a beautiful song about it. I became bitter and resentful and I blamed God. I know I said that I didn't blame anyone, but I feel like I did. I think I didn't want to blame anyone because I knew it was wrong, but deep down, I felt like I had been cheated.

"When I came in here today, I thought about my miscarriages and how sad I was about losing my babies. But I don't want to lose my relationship with God over it because without Him, I'd really be a mess. I'd be hopeless," I said, wiping my face with tissue.

Dr. Wilson grabbed my free hand and said, "It sounds like you needed to mourn. That's what I heard when you were crying. A woman in mourning. You lost something that was a part of you, and it's okay to feel sad, hurt, and disappointed about it. It's okay to cry over it. You had to let it out because if not, it would have continued to eat you up on the inside."

I gazed up at Eric who had also shed a few tears in the process. "Baby," I said, "I'm so sorry for holding a grudge against you and your daughter. I love you with all of my heart, and I can't imagine losing you. And I love Jonelle. God has given us so much to be thankful for. If I never have a child of my own, I thank Him for giving me the opportunity to know motherhood by having a hand in raising Jonelle. I really mean that."

Eric grinned at me. "I know you do, babe. And I'm sorry for not understanding how much you lost with the miscarriages, and not comforting you as much as I should have. Now I get why having sex has been so difficult for you. And as much as I miss touching you, I don't want you to hurt anymore. So I am willing to wait for you, as long as it takes."

I stood up from my seat and rushed over to my husband to hug him. We held each other close and cried.

After the session, upon the recommendation of Dr. Wilson, I decided to go and get a massage. Dr. Wilson said that counseling and dealing with deeply rooted emotional issues could take a toll on the physical body. She suggested that I consider taking out a little time for pampering. There was a day spa in the area that accepted walk-in clients, so I hiked the few blocks over to the spa and selected an 80-minute, hot stone therapy massage.

My masseuse was a woman name Dionne. She had short, somewhat spiky hair, and a demeanor that immediately let me know that she was a no-nonsense kind of woman. She greeted me in the waiting area, and led me back to a private treatment room. She explained the process and asked if I had any areas of my body that needed special attention.

"No, not really. I'm just wanting to relax. I've been going through a lot of stress lately, and have been told that I need some pampering," I responded.

She left the room for a few minutes while I undressed and eased—face down—onto the massage bed, sliding under the thin white sheets and blankets as Dionne had instructed. She knocked on the door before re-entering the room, then came in and started to prepare the smooth, black, rocks for the massage.

Dionne began massaging my back, first without the stones, then slowly introducing them to my skin. The heat for the stones penetrated through my back, sending a warm sensation throughout my body. The caress of her touch felt amazing, but I guess I wasn't relaxing enough because in mid-knead she stopped and said, "Um unn, um umm. Let go. Um unn, let go."

I was confused. Let go of what? She continued to rub my back, and I assumed that maybe she was trying to communicate to me that I was tense and needed to unwind more. I tried to breathe out and loosen my body. Yet, a few minutes later, she paused once again and said, "Um unn. Let go. Let go."

Was this woman crazy? What was she talking about? I didn't want to ruin my massage, so I ignored her remarks, and once again tried to relax and enjoy the massage. A couple of minutes passed before she was at it again. "Let go. Um unn. You have to let go. No. Um unn."

I was about to flip over and ask her what in the devil she was talking about, when she said, "Come on, sweetie. You have to let go."

And then it hit me. Hard. She could feel all of the tension in my body. All of the stress and pain I had been carrying had my muscles all knotted up, and until I let go, until I truly relaxed, she could not do her job. I was trying to control everything, even the massage. Just like Dr. Wilson and even Eric, the people who were in my life to help me could not assist me until I completely and fully let go.

So I did.

I took another deep breathe and let it out, imagining myself letting go of all of my hurts, disappointments, sadness, and grief. Dionne continue to massage me and said, "There you go. That's it. Yes, that's it."

Once again, fresh tears overtook me. I wanted to stop them, and even considered holding back, embarrassed about crying during a spa treatment, but letting go meant giving up the façades. So I cried. I thought Dionne would feel uncomfortable with my tears, but instead she said, "Um hmm, let it out. There you go. Let it out."

And I did.

Dr. Wilson and Dionne were right. It was time to mourn, let go, and let it out.

Lesson 17: A Time to Build Up

A time to kill and a time to heal; a time to tear down and a time to build up. (Ecclesiastes 3:3)

Your seed will I establish forever, and build up your throne to all generations. Selah. (Psalm 89:4)

Dr. Wilson

Once again, I attended sunrise prayer, breakfast, and the couples' class without my mate. I still had peace that God was working on my behalf, even if I didn't know how. The couples' class was exceptionally inspiring on Wednesday, and it seemed everyone in the tent felt the power of Lydia's lesson. The song "Tis So Sweet" perfectly matched my feelings. I was going through a cloudy place in my life, but holding on to Jesus and trusting Him was a very sweet experience. I found myself praising God for keeping me sane during such a trying time.

My counseling sessions for the day were full of surprises. When I hit the beach at 4:00 p.m. to self-debrief, I was overwhelmed. God was definitely moving that day. I closed my eyes and tried to contain my enthusiasm as I replayed my day.

Eric and Amber. That session was heavy. I was so shaken up after my meeting with Amber and Eric that I had to take five. If I was a smoker, I would have been out in front of the hotel, puffing on a cigarette or two. Instead, I went into the bathroom, splashed cold water on my face, and prayed. I was already a mess over my own marriage, so watching Amber grieve over her miscarriages was brutal. But I'll tell you one thing, those two know how to make up. They genuinely love each other. Watching them hug and cry together was a bigger tearjerker than watching a movie on the Hallmark Channel. It took me singing in my mind the lyrics to Mary J. Blige's "I'm Not Gonna Cry" to keep me from joining in with them for a group hug. Now that would have been really weird. They seemed to be reaching their goals in counseling, but I couldn't say that I had anything to do with it. No matter who or what was behind their development, I was happy to see them healing.

Carl and Kelly. These two were changing right in front of my eyes. At the beginning, if there was a couple that I thought would not make it successfully through counseling, it was Carl and Kelly, but they were proving me wrong.

"So we did our list together like you told us," Kelly said, "and we came up with some compromises that we both feel good about."

"Okay. I'm listening. Let me hear them," I responded.

"I agreed to pay a couple of the smaller bills each month like the cable bill and the insurance on both of our cars. Those two bills together are about two hundred-fifty dollars. I already help out with the mortgage on our home, but I can afford to pay an extra two bills if it would reduce the financial stress on Carl. And he agreed that when he earned bigger commission check than normal, he would take me out shopping or treat me to the spa," Kelly said.

"That's wonderful. It sounds like a very simple compromise that will benefit the both of you," I said. "So what else you got?"

"Well," Carl said, "I agreed to give Kelly every other Saturday off to do what she wants to while I take care of the girls' needs. So I'll take them where they need to go, feed them, and whatnot and Kelly can have a break or as she calls it, some 'me time.' I'm also going to start cooking on Wednesday nights unless I have a closing. But I usually leave work early on Wednesdays, so for the most part it shouldn't be a problem. And I'm going to try to be a little more mindful of picking up behind myself. I'm not promising a complete 180 degree change, but I will make more of an effort if it will make life a little easier for her. She agreed to stop running away from the house, to not go out to the clubs so much, and to wear clothing that is less revealing, so I'm cool with that."

"Alright! I am really proud of you two. If I had gold star stickers, I would give you both one for today."

We all laughed about it. I could tell by the way they were grinning at each other, that they were also pleased with themselves.

"So what's our homework for tonight?" Kelly asked at the end of the session.

Well what do you know? She actually liked having homework. So I gave them something to do that I knew she wouldn't complain about. "Tonight, I want the two of you to go do something fun together. You are on South Beach, so enjoy yourself. You both deserve it."

"We can do that!" Kelly said excitedly.

Franklin and Tamela. After yesterday's session with the Days, I felt a closer connection to them. I appreciated the fact that they took their set aside time to help me deal with my own issues. I definitely had never had a client do that before. I also was grateful that they had not spilled the beans about my relationship woes to the rest of the group. Yes, we had discussed me becoming more honest about my imperfections with the world, but I was in the middle of a job and not yet ready to start blabbing all of my shortcomings. It would have been counterproductive to all of the good work I was doing with the other couples.

I noticed when Franklin and Tamela came into the session that they were smiling really hard at me. I smiled back, chopping it up to our newfound bond. A minute later, there was a knock at the door of the counseling suite. I presumed it was either the Woods needing a quick word with me, or one of my earlier couples who had left something behind and was coming back to retrieve it. I looked around and didn't see any misplaced belongings, so I shrugged, stood up, walked over to the door, and opened it.

Lem walked in.

My bottom lip hit the floor. Franklin and Tamela were still smiling. What in the world was going on?

My initial thought was to hurry him out of the room. I was in a counseling session with a couple. It was very unprofessional to have my husband bust up in the middle of me meeting with clients. Then I thought about it. I had spent the entire previous session talking with these clients about the struggles in my marriage. They already knew our problems, so I didn't have to hide behind a professional demeanor.

I glanced over at the Days and said, "Sorry for the interruption. If you'll excuse me for a moment, I'll just go into the hallway to talk to my husband."

"You can talk in here, "Tamela insisted. "Come on, Lem. Come sit down with us."

Lem followed her directions and sat down next to her on the sofa as if they were one big, happy family. I was confused and a bit irritated by Mrs. Day inviting Lem to join our session. Yet, I took my seat across from them since I was the only one who seemed to have an issue with the situation.

"Hi, Andrea," Lem said.

It was at that moment that I realized that I had not greeted him at the door and we hadn't spoken to each other since he'd entered the room. "Hi, Lem," I said, feeling awkward and guilty. "Wha-What are you doing here? I thought you went back to Rochester."

"I never left."

All eyes turned to look at me, awaiting my response.

What? He never left? How could that be? I hadn't seen him in days.

"I don't understand. What do you mean you never left?"

Lem peered at Franklin who then spoke up on his behalf. "Lem's been staying with us. Well, not actually with us, but we put him up in another room in a hotel down the block. We ran into him the night you all had the fight. He was in the lobby looking as if he had nowhere to go. We sat down and talked to him about what happened and we encouraged him to stay so that you two could work on your marriage."

I was dumbfounded. Not only had my husband never left South Beach, but the Days were in cahoots with him. It now made sense why they were so forceful about getting me to talk about my marriage problems. I didn't know whether to hug them or to chastise them for not telling me the truth.

Tamela must have detected my apprehension because she said, "We're sorry for keeping this information from you, but Lem made us promise not to tell you until he sorted out how to come back and work things out with you. After yesterday's discussion with you, we suggested that he come with us today and talk to you."

So I had been setup. As much as I hated being left out of the loop, it was probably for the best. The time alone had allowed me to do some thinking and make some hard decisions. I'd decided that I wanted my marriage, so I couldn't be mad about God's way of working out the details.

"I see. Thank you for helping," I said. "Lem, I'm glad to see you. I'm happy that you didn't leave."

"Me too. I'm happy that I didn't leave too," he said. "Andrea, I've been doing a lot of thinking over these past two days. At first,

I was so angry with you. I couldn't believe how much you disrespected me. In all of our years of being together, you never once talked to me like that. I thought you had turned into this evil person, and all I could say to myself is, 'This isn't my wife.' I tried to imagine myself being married to someone who would treat me so badly and I couldn't do it. That's not the kind of marriage we had or that I wanted us to have. But then I started to think about my part in the problem and what I did wrong. I guess I just didn't think that making that one decision to pay my employees using our money would have such a negative impact on our marriage. I just wanted to square them away and have one less worry. I feel really guilty knowing that they are struggling to get by when we have so much. I just wanted to do what I could do to make sure they got paid for their work.

"But it was wrong for me to put their needs in front of my own family's needs without discussing it with you first. I knew when I was writing out the checks that you'd be upset, but then I thought you'd get over it and we had enough money to be okay. But that's not how it all worked out. I took you for granted and my assumptions were incorrect. As much as I still think that you could have handled the situation a little better and not resorted to belittling me, I also take full responsibility for my actions that put us in this predicament. I apologize."

I gazed into his eyes. He was sincere. Like I said, Lem didn't talk much, but when he did, he meant what he said. "Thank you, Lem, for admitting that. I needed to hear it. I'm sorry too. I should have never said some of the mean things that came out of my mouth. I knew they were foul when I said them. I know better than that. Franklin and Tamela have helped me come to realize that my position as a psychologist makes it hard for me to just be a regular person who makes mistakes in relationships. I think I took out on you my frustration with feeling like I need to be perfect. I just wanted to do the wrong thing on purpose for once.

It was silly and I'm sorry that I hurt your feelings. I constantly lecture my clients about not being authentic, but here I am doing the same thing. I promise that I'm going to start working on breaking out of this box I've placed my own self in."

Lem let out a heavy sigh as if relieved. "I want us to participate in the rest of the marriage retreat together, so that we can get our marriage back on track."

I glanced over at the Days who were still smiling at me. "Okay." I was fortunate. I had my man back.

Then Lem burst my bubble. "But I'm not coming back to the room. At least not yet."

My heart plummeted. Did he build me up just to break me down? "Why not?"

"I just think we need to give it some time."

I wanted to fuss about it. I wanted him back with me, back in my—our room immediately. I didn't want to sleep another night without him by my side. For the last time, I looked over at the Days. This time they weren't smiling. I think they were bracing themselves for my reaction. I was spoiled, but I wasn't foolish—anymore. "If that's what you want. Okay."

Jordan and Sarah. By the time the Jordan and Sarah's session began, I was emotionally drained. Being on the other side—the client side—of marriage counseling was exhausting. I was glad that Lem and I had our apology meeting, but I still had to get through two more couples before I could process it all. Thankfully, both couples were fairly low key.

I introduced Jordan and Sarah to the final piece of The Awareness Wheel—actions. "After you've talked about your wants, it's time to talk about actions. This is somewhat the solution part of communication. Sometimes all we do is complain without offering any practical solutions for the problem. In actions, there are three sub-actions: current, past, and future. You want to identify what actions you've done in the past related to the issue, what you've recently or current are doing, and what you plan to do in the future. So back to our example of Sarah wanting to go out to dinner, it might sound like this: 'In the past, I've begged you to take me out and sulked when you refused. Currently, I just stopped asking all together. In the future, I will ask you again, but if you say no, I will go out by myself or with one of my female friends.' Got it? You two ready to try it?"

As with the past two sessions, they both were able to express their actions verbally with their selected problems. I had them walk through all five sections of the wheel and they were able to do so successfully. Since we only had two more sessions left, I planned to have them use a new problem at the next session to practice their new communication skills. During the final session, I would review all we had covered in counseling, like I intended to do with all of my clients.

Martin and Lydia. The Woods had their spiritual list out and ready at the start of our session. We talked for a while about them both feeling a strong calling to teach Bible study courses related to real life issues as they had been doing with the Wife 101 and Husband 101 courses. They shared that they wanted to expand this ministry to tackle other issues in Christian living like parenting and single living. They were already plotting a Singles conference in the near future, but they suspected that it would be another year or two before they could actually implement it because they wanted to get the right people on staff for it, as well as open it up to Christian singles around the country. It was their grandest idea to date, so they were taking their time to pull all of the pieces together.

At the close of our session, I felt it was only right to let them in on what had been going on in my marriage. They had paid me to be the professional at their event, and even though Lem and I were back on speaking terms, I didn't want to keep any major secrets from them that could have impacted my work with the couples at the retreat.

"Mr. and Mrs. Woods, there's something I need to tell you. I've been wanting to share this with you over the last couple of days, but I wasn't sure how to say it and not alarm you," I admitted.

"What's wrong, honey?" Lydia asked, looking very concerned.

"It's like this—Lem and I have had some marital problems since we've been at this retreat. It got so bad that he left, and I thought that he went back to New York, but come to find out that he really was staying at another hotel on the strip with the help of Pastor and First Lady Day. Earlier today, we met and talked, and it appears that we are on the road to reconciliation, but I needed to be honest with at least you two about our situation. I realize that you hired me to help the couples on the retreat, but I am not sure how much assistance I've given them when I've been consumed with my own troubles. If you don't want to pay the rest of the balance at the end of the retreat, I understand, and won't hold it against you."

Lydia looked at Martin and they began to laugh. I didn't think I said anything funny so I stared at them in confusion. "Sorry, love," Lydia said when she noticed my serious expression. "Martin and I suspected something was wrong between you and your husband when he sort of disappeared, but that is your own business and it was up to you to share it with us if you wanted to. And you've been doing a terrific job. Martin and I were just talking this morning about how much our counseling sessions with you have helped us put our children leaving home and this new phase of our lives in the proper perspective. If your time with the other couples is anything like your time with us, we know you are making a difference. We would never refuse to finish paying you."

"That's a relief," I said, more about their confidence that I was doing my job than the money.

Martin continued to laugh. "I think it's hilarious that Pastor Franklin and Tamela stashed your husband at another hotel. That sounds like something they would do."

I chuckled at the thought of them smuggling my husband away behind my back. "I'm glad you're getting a kick out of it because I almost fell out sick from worrying over where he went. He wasn't answering my calls and he would call my hotel room out of the blue and barely say a word. It was very stressful for me."

"Well, praise God that it is all working out for your good," Lydia said. "I knew the enemy would have some tricks up his sleeve here in South Beach for our couples, I just didn't think our psychologist might be one of the victims. That goes to show you that no one is immune and that evil is always on its job. We have to put on the whole armor, all of us."

"I'm so happy that I serve a God who is strong and mighty, and who gives us power over all of the power of the enemy," Martin added, jubilantly.

"Amen to that," I said.

I got back to my hotel room around quarter to five. I had a message on the hotel room's phone. It was Lem, asking me to have dinner with him at the restaurant in front of the Beacon. He told me to meet him at six, as if he knew I would agree. Yeah, I would.

I showered and changed into a short, white and pink dress with white shoes. I wondered if the no white after Labor Day rule applied on South Beach where it was summer all year long. If it did, I was going to break the rule repeatedly, because I had brought a few white outfits I had yet to wear. I threw on jewelry and squirted myself with my favorite Chanel perfume before leaving the room.

When I arrived downstairs at 5:55 p.m., Lem was already there, seated at a table, waiting for me. As I sauntered up to the table, he stood like a gentleman, kissed me on my forehead, and pulled out my chair. All I could think was, why did I ever give this man a hard time? He had made a dumb mistake, but he was still one of the good guys.

Dinner was fantastic. Everything from the food, to the live music, to the conversation was delightful. That was the thing about breaking up. If you had a solid relationship from the start, the making up part was so rewarding. Lem told me how he had spent the majority of the past two days locked up in his hotel room. In addition to being down and wanting to be alone, he didn't want to run the risk of bumping into me or anyone else from the retreat. Outside of going out to grab food or stretch his legs, he had remained indoors.

While we were dining, Eric and Amber walked past us on the sidewalk. Both of them did a double take when they saw Lem with me. I guess they had been wondering what rock he'd been hiding underneath. They spoke to the both of us and continued on down the strip, probably heading out to dinner as well. We also saw Jordan and Sarah who were so engrossed in talking to each other that they didn't even notice us as they passed by. It appeared the Couples Communication lessons were really helping them. I inwardly wanted to high five myself.

After dinner, Lem and I took a long walk on the beach. We didn't talk much during our stroll, we simply enjoyed each other's presence. On the way back to the hotel, we bought ice cream. Lem walked me all of the way to my room and opened the door for me, before planting a sweet kiss on my lips, saying goodbye, and leaving me alone with dreamy thoughts about him.

Lesson 18: Offense Sells Tickets, Defense Wins Games

And take the helmet of salvation, and the sword of the Spirit, which is the word of God. (Ephesians 6:17)

Amber

Eric and I took the rest of Wednesday easy. It had been extremely draining for us, getting all of our emotions out. We both felt empty and depleted, but in a good way. We decided to spend a good portion of the day on the beach relaxing. I read a book while he played another game of water football with Martin and some other men. After swimming, we took a nap, then went out to dinner. I was taken aback to see Dr. Wilson dining with her husband in front of the hotel. I hadn't seen him with her or around at all in days. I was starting to think that an emergency had come up and he had to leave. It was nice to see this was not the case, and they were still enjoying the retreat together.

On Thursday, Eric and I woke up feeling lighter and more energized. Sunrise prayer and breakfast went smoothly, and we were both amped for the couples' class. Martin was set-up to lead the class, so we arranged our beach chairs as close as possible to the front, and nestled in for a good lesson.

"Today is Day Six of Battle Boot Camp. Tomorrow will be your final day of training," Martin began. "We are down to the last two components of your military gear—your head gear and your weapon. Let's take a moment to read Ephesians 6:17. Read it quietly to yourself."

In a rush to get to the tent, Eric forgot to bring his Bible, so I opened mine to the correct scripture and placed it between the two of us so that we both could follow along.

When Martin noticed that we were all ready, he continued. "Again, most of you probably have the Kings James version, but I am going to read from the Amplified version. 'And take the helmet of salvation and the sword that the Spirit wields, which is the Word of God.' So this verse is telling us that our head gear is the helmet of salvation, and our weapon of choice is a sword which is God's Word. Now bear with me for a moment as I attempt to break this down."

"Take your time," Pastor Day said, and I had to stifle my laugh. Did everyone have to sound like an old church mother?

Martin continued. "In war, you have to protect your head, because your skull contains your brain, and next to your heart, your brain is the most essential organ in your body. Your brain is the control center of your body; it send messages to every part of your system to tell it what to do. It also controls your thoughts and feelings. In a physical fight, if your opponent destroyed or even damaged your brain, it would more than likely be fatal. The same is true for spiritual warfare; if the enemy can destroy or damage your brain spiritually, you will more than likely die a spiritual death.

"Therefore, we need this helmet to protect our head, to protect our brain, and the particular helmet we need is salvation. Salvation is your acceptance of God's grace and mercy; it's your confessed belief that Jesus Christ died for your sins and arose from the grave to give you everlasting life through Him. The one guaranteed tactic that the devil will always try to use against you is attempting to keep you from salvation or rob you of your faith in salvation. He'll tell you, 'All religions are the same. As long as you believe in a god, you're okay. You don't have to believe in Jesus.' Or he'll say, 'You're not saved or you can't be saved. All of the horrible things you've done? You'll always be a sinner. God can't save you.' And then once he's weakened you in the area of salvation, he'll move on and encourage you to continue sinning and hurting yourself, or even to kill yourself. And for those of you who he can't get to believe that salvation isn't yours, he'll switch his strategy and try to confuse you by telling you other lies about yourself or God."

I heard Eric say, "Amen." It was a turn-on to see him so excited about God's Word.

"So you see, we need this helmet, this salvation, to protect our minds from the devil's lies because remember, he's the father of lies. But we also need a weapon, something to use to attack back. Now, up until this point, we've only been discussing the parts of our godly armor that are used for defensive purposes, items that will protect us in battle. But now the Word shifts and tells us we also need to have a plan of attack, an offensive tool so that we can fight back. That instrument is the Word of God, our Bibles, God's commandments, the Word God has spoken into our lives. Oh, this is getting too good. Y'all bear with me while I try to contain myself," Martin said to the group.

"Take your time," Eric said, and I almost fell out.

Martin waved his hand in praise before continuing. "You have to make sure that you have the right weapon. This verse doesn't say anything about the grenade of an attitude, the gun of anger, or even the pistol of passiveness. No. Our offensive weapon is the sword of the Spirit which is the Word of God. So when the enemy starts attacking you with lies, confusion, and havoc, you can fight back with God's Word. When he tells you that you've done too much and can't be saved, you tell him, 'I am saved by faith through grace, not of myself. It is a gift from God—Ephesians 2:8.' When he says, 'You've messed up too many times. God isn't going to forgive you this time,' you tell him, 'A just man falls seven times and rises again—Psalm 24:16. My God removes my sins from me, as far as the east is from the west; He remembers my sins no more—Psalm 103:12 and Isaiah 43:25.' When he tries to hit you with confusion, tell him, 'God is not the author of confusion, but of peace—I Corinthians 14:33.' When you know the Word, stand firmly on it, and use it in battle, the enemy gets to running. 'Submit yourself to God. Resist the devil and he shall flee—James 4:7.' Are you all starting to get it?"

"Yes!" the group responded in unison.

"Good," Martin said. "I'm going to end this lesson with this analogy. Those of us who are into sports have a saying, 'Offense sells tickets, defense wins games.' In looking at the full armor of God, there are a total of six items we must put on, but of those six items, five of them are defensive tools and only one is offensive. Why do you think this is so?"

Martin became silent for a second as if he was waiting for an answer, although we all knew the question was rhetorical. I swore to myself if someone else said 'take your time' I would have gotten up and straight walked out of the tent. There was no way I'd be able to hold my laughter again. Luckily for me, no one spoke.

Martin put down his Bible, then said, "When you watch an action movie and the hero is getting ready to go into battle, you often see him or her gearing up with a bunch of offensive weapons. They might have several guns, loads of bullets, a few knives, a grenade, and whatnot. But that's the movies. This isn't a movie or a game; this is real life, this is our spiritual life which impacts our physical life. We have to be smart. In the movies, the hero has no bulletproof jacket or any armor, but somehow magically fights and kills fifty armed men and comes out alive, without a scratch, or sometimes with a minor surface wound. Really?"

He shook his head. "We must understand the importance of protecting ourselves so that we can come out alive. The saying, 'Offense sell tickets, defense wins games,' often refers to the belief that having a good offensive line will attract crowds, but ultimately, a good defensive line will win the game. In football, people love the star quarterback who can throw the ball skillfully to his teammate waiting in the end zone, or even the guy who runs the ball himself in for a touchdown. A great offensive line will get people to come to every game, excited about the show. But it's the defensive lines that the players and coaches have to be worried about. Because no matter how good of an offensive line, if they can't score because they can't get past the defense, they can't win. And see, when you get down to the playoffs or better yet, the Superbowl, by then the teams are usually evenly matched, especially in offensive lines. It all comes down to which team's defensive line can make the most offensive stops to keep the other team from scoring. The team with the better performing defense is most likely to win the game."

Martin was talking about football. I looked around and noticed all of the men seemed heavily engrossed, while all of the women appeared to be in deep concentration, trying hard to follow his line of reasoning.

"This idea can be projected onto spiritual warfare," he said. "The reason there is more defensive armor than offensive, five-to-one, is because your defense will get you the victory. If the enemy can't get past your protective armor, he can't defeat you. And while he's struggling with tactics that aren't working against your defense, you use your one offensive tool to score on him and win the game. Remember, the battle is for your soul. The enemy's goal is to claim your soul by trying to kill you, steal from you, and destroy you. But if you're suited up and ready, not only can you cause him to fail at his goal of winning your soul, you might also win a few other souls for Christ in the process."

Lesson 19: A Time to Embrace

A time to cast away stones, and a time to gather stones together;
a time to embrace, and a time to refrain from embracing.
(Ecclesiastes 3:5)

His left hand is under my head, and his right hand does embrace
me. (Song of Solomon 2:6)

Eric

I was so hyped following the couples' class. I loved the sports examples Martin often used to break down the Bible. Offense sells tickets, defense wins games. That was priceless! I had heard and even used that saying a zillion times, but now it would mean something entirely different. From this point on, I would make sure that my family had a strong defensive end. It was my job to protect my wife and child. I would no longer allow the enemy to beat us because our defensive strategies were weak. No, we would be ready, every day, every time.

Amber and I went into our counseling session ready for whatever Dr. Wilson had for us. I had never attended therapy in my life, and truth be told, I had started the process a bit reluctantly. Nonetheless, now that we were near the end of our seven sessions, I felt empowered by our time in counseling and wished we could continue going once we got back home. But I would never admit that to Amber. She would have us working with some nutcase. If I couldn't work with Dr. Wilson anymore, I didn't want to go . . . unless we were back in a situation that required intervention.

Thursday's session was way less dramatic than Wednesday. Dr. Wilson told us that because our time was coming to a close, she didn't want to bring up any new issues and leave us emotionally untied when we returned to Atlanta. So she was going into more of a review mode with us for the final two sessions.

"So where are you two with the whole physical affection issue?" Dr. Wilson asked toward the end of the session. "I hoped that you all would get the chance to at least become more affectionate during this retreat, such as cuddling at night. Yesterday, it was great to see you two hugging, so that is some level of progress. Anything else?"

Amber glanced at me as if to question which of us should answer the question. I decided to take the lead, and said, "We actually did cuddle last night."

"Really?" Dr. Wilson asked, her face lit up like a Christmas tree.

Amber nodded shyly. "Yes, we did. It was such an emotional day that I really needed to feel him close to me. So he held me as we slept. It was really nice. I didn't realize how much I missed being close to him in that way."

"That is superb! I am truly happy for you all. Wow," Dr. Wilson said. "How was the experience for you, Eric?"

"It was great," I answered. "I also missed being able to touch her in that way. It felt really good."

"You guys have really made my day with this news. I hope that you continue to grow more comfortable with physical affection. Remember, you don't have to rush it. You want it to be authentic so that when Amber is actually ready to have sex again, she can completely relax and prayerfully, it won't be painful."

The thought of Amber and I rekindling our sexual relationship brought a smile to my face. I knew I would have to be patient and that it might not happen for a while, but we were definitely moving in that direction and I knew we would get there. Until then, I would appreciate what she was willing to offer, even if it was just a hug or a kiss.

That was what I told myself while we were still in the counseling session with Dr. Wilson. However, when Amber came out of the bathroom later that night, dressed in a fiery red lace teddy, with her hair down over her shoulders, and some sparkly high heels that she had to buy out here on SoBe because I doubted they sold them anywhere else in the world, I was a goner.

My jaw dropped and I was temporarily speechless.

"You like?" she asked, toying with me.

I nodded my head like I had no brain.

She giggled, walked closer to me, and kissed me gently on each of my cheeks. "Eric, I'm ready," she said.

Thank you, Jesus!

Lesson 20: A Time to Love

A time to love, and a time to hate; a time of war, and a time of peace. (Ecclesiastes 3:8)

There is no fear in love; but perfect love casteth out fear: because fear hath torment. He that feareth is not made perfect in love. (I John 4:18)

Dr. Wilson

As promised, Lem attended sunrise prayer with me, breakfast, and the couples' class. When you're married and you get used to doing a lot of activities with your spouse, you forget how blessed you are and what it's like to be alone, until for some reason, you have to be alone. After going solo for a couple of days, being back with my hubby was bliss. I enjoyed him so much that I hated to leave his side to conduct my counseling session, but I had to do what I had to do. The positive part was that Lem and I met up midday for lunch as well as in the evening for dinner.

Following my last appointment for the day, I rushed over to the beach to self-debrief. I didn't want to spend too much time replaying my day because I was excited about meeting up with my husband. But for the sake of having a clear mind, I quickly ran through each therapy session.

Eric and Amber. After a tearful session the day prior, Mr. and Mrs. Hayes came to their second to last therapy appointment with spectacular news. They had cuddled. Alright, in a normal situation, cuddling wasn't a big deal. But in the grand scheme of their lives, cuddling was a major development.

As a psychologist, I was amazed at the progress of all of my clients. Each one of them, with of course the exception of the Days, were working towards their goals. In brief therapy, a clinician hopes that growth will occur over such a short period of time, but often, even small objectives are never met. I knew that it was nothing short of God's hands that were on this group, working in and through them.

Carl and Kelly. I had given the Bradfords an easy assignment— to go out and have a good time together. Since they'd been on South Beach, I knew that Kelly had went out a few times, but I wasn't sure if they had done anything truly enjoyable as a couple. They came to our session, full of exciting stories about their time out.

"After lunch, Amber and I went shopping for a couple of hours," Kelly said. "When we returned, Carl and I found a water sports adventure company and we went jet skiing and parasailing. It was so cool."

"Yeah, I've been wanting to Jet Ski forever, but never made the time," Carl added. "It was a blast. Kelly kept trying to race me, but she couldn't keep up with the king."

Kelly punched Carl lightly on the arm. "Whatever. You were cheating. Dr. Wilson, he cheated so much. He was splashing water on me, knowing I didn't want to get my hair wet."

"That's what I don't understand about women. Why would you get in the water and try not to get your hair wet? Doesn't make sense to me. If you don't want to get wet, stay on land," Carl said.

Kelly rolled her eyes. "Anyway, so we had dinner and then last night, we went to this outdoor concert. It was some live bands performing. I don't even know who they were, but it was still fun."

"It sounds like you all had a great time," I said. "See, neither of you have to be 'old.' You both are proving that age is a state of mind and that you can still enjoy life to the fullest in your forties without having to revert back to being a teeny-bopper."

"You're right, Dr. Wilson," Kelly said. "I had more fun with my husband doing grown folks stuff yesterday than all of the times I went out clubbing with a bunch of young kids. Thanks for showing me that my life isn't over."

Franklin and Tamela. Lem attended the Days' counseling session, but this time, I knew he would be there. We decided to use the time to figure out what we were going to do about our financial situation.

"I'm willing to pay your car note to keep it from being repossessed," I offered.

"I can't let you do that," Lem said. "You've already made a lot of sacrifices because of my bad decision."

"You have to let me do it. If you don't, not only will you lose the truck and we will be out of a second vehicle, but it will also negatively affect your credit which will hurt us even more," I said.

Lem sighed. "I can't believe that I messed up this bad. What was I thinking?"

"There's no use in crying over spilled milk. I'm just glad that God has blessed me with the extra money to fix this," I said.

"So, Lem," Tamela said. "I hear your wife offering to help you, but I haven't heard what you're going to do in return. Compromise goes both ways. What are you offering?"

I loved that woman. I could see how she had captured the pastor's heart.

Lem thought about the question for a few minutes, then responded, "I can make a promise that I will no longer take jobs without getting paid up front. From now on, a deposit of half the total must be made before I start the contract, and the rest must be paid at the halfway point."

"That's a start," Franklin said. "What else?"

These two drove a hard bargain. I sat back and sucked it all in.

Lem laughed and said, "Okay, I hear you all. When I get paid from this job, not only will I pay my wife back in full, I will also take her out, anywhere she wants to go. And I will give her an extra five hundred dollars to put in her savings account, sort of like interest and as a thank you gift for cleaning up my mistake."

"And?" Tamela pressed.

Lem smiled. "And, I will never again make another important decision without consulting her first."

Franklin and Tamela looked at each other, then at me. "What do you think, Mrs. Wilson," Tamela asked.

I pretended like I was mulling over the details, then said, "I think we have a deal."

Jordan and Sarah. The Larks session was simple. I had them each pick a new issue to discuss, and to go around The Awareness Wheel, communicating their views on the issue. Both of them reported feeling better about talking to one another when there was a problem. They seemed to be really getting the hang of expressing themselves fully and correctly.

"These sessions have been wonderful for us," Sarah admitted. "We've been talking so much more now that we know how to say things in a manner that won't offend the other person. Jordan has also let down his guard a little and we've been able to take advantage of some of the tourist attractions. Jordan still doesn't feel too comfortable in big crowds so we've avoided congested places, but we have done boat tours of Star Island and the Everglades, and even went to Zoo Miami. It's been a lot of fun."

"Yeah, it has been," Jordan said. "I don't think I've enjoyed myself like this in a long time."

"That's really good to hear. Hopefully, as you continue to work on your anxiety issues, you'll be able to get out more back home and enjoy living with your family."

I made a note to pull up a few psychiatrist in Atlanta that I could recommend to Jordan about his PTSD. Officially, he hadn't been diagnosed with the disorder. Because I wasn't seeing him long term or billing his health care provider, I didn't give him a diagnosis, but I would write up my concerns and submit them to whomever he decided to go to for more long-term treatment.

Martin and Lydia. My session with the Woods was also very light and casual. We talked more about their ministry plans and about how well the marriage retreat had turned out. They asked me for an overall assessment of how well the various couples did in counseling, and I was able to report to them that I had seen growth and positive improvement in everyone.

Before they left my counseling suite, they asked me one final question.

"Dr. Wilson," Martin said, "we have a huge favor to ask of you."

"I'm listening," I responded.

"It's okay if you say no, but I think it would be very powerful if you and Lem share your testimony with the group tomorrow during the couples' class," he said.

"Our testimony?" I asked, unsure of what he meant.

Lydia spoke up. "What Martin is trying to say is that we thought what you told us about what happened between your husband and yourself during this retreat was inspiring. Not that your marital problems were inspiring, but how God had a plan to bring you two back together, and how when you were here to help others, the enemy was trying to tear down your marriage."

"Sometimes when we teach these lessons, they can come across like theories. Ideas but not real life examples," Martin said. "But your story is very real, and we think it would bless others to know about it. Now, we completely understand if you don't want anyone else to know. You reserve the right to say no. But we hope you'll take this as an opportunity to really help the few couples who aren't aware of the situation. They need to know that no couple is perfect, not even those of us here to help."

"We've shared some of our stories with these couples in other classes we've taught," Lydia said. "Most of them know us. Sometimes it is just good to hear from someone new, someone else that they respect and trust."

I thought about it. Although I had no plans to share the details of my marriage with people who I considered my clients, there were only three couples at the retreat who didn't already know. If it would really help their marriages, it might not be a bad idea.

"I want to help, but this is not a decision I can make alone. I need to discuss it with my husband first. If he is in agreement, I'm willing to share it with the group," I said. "We'll call you this evening and let you know."

I finished my day's review and made my way back to the hotel. Lem was waiting for me in the lobby. I found myself smiling super hard the moment I saw him. He was smiling too.

He followed me to the room where I changed for dinner. While I put on my shoes, I told him about the proposal from Martin and Lydia, to share our testimony. I didn't know how he would take the request, but he stunned me when he said, "Okay, let's do it."

"You're okay with it?" I asked.

"Sure. If it will help the others, why not? You love to help people with their marriages. This week, others have helped us. I think if we keep paying it forward, we will keep getting it back when we need it most."

That was another trait I loved about my husband. He understood the law of reciprocity.

Lesson 21: Don't Sleep

Praying always with all prayer and supplication in the Spirit, and watching thereunto with all perseverance and supplication for all saints. (Ephesians 6:18)

Eric

On Friday, I had a pep in my step. There is a verse in the Bible that talks about how when God finally blesses you that He'll make you remember your struggle no more, or something like that. I didn't know the actual passage, but I could confirm that it was true. My night with Amber had been so amazing that I couldn't even remember all of the cold nights before it. I couldn't believe that after three months of shooting me down, she finally let me make love to her. And the best part was that I could tell that she was enjoying it as much as I was. Man, God was good!

As joyous as I was about being intimate with my wife, I hated that the retreat was ending. Today was our last day and it felt so bittersweet. Every moment of the retreat wasn't good, but overall, it was exactly what we needed, when we needed it.

Martin was teaching the final couples' class and I knew he would leave us with something deep to take back home.

"Wow," Martin said. "We're at Day Seven, the final day of the retreat. I am sure that this experience has been life changing for all of us. That's the reality of development; in order to grow we have to be stretched beyond what's normal and comfortable. So tonight, we have a special evening planned for you all. Instead of the regular free time during dinner, we are all going to spend the evening together on a private yacht, enjoying dinner and a recommitment ceremony. All of you are required to participate in the dinner cruise, but each of you will have a choice of whether or not you want to take part in the recommitment ceremony. It will basically be a renewal of vows, but instead of all of the fuss over a wedding and who to invite, this ceremony will focus on you, your mate, and God. So often weddings are about everything and everybody except the vow being made. By recommitting yourself here, you and your spouse will be able to keep your attention on only what matters most. If you decided not to participate, that's fine. No one will judge you. It just means that there are some things that you and your mate need to work on.

"During this week, we've aimed to educate you and train you on how to be ready and prepared for spiritual warfare. We started off identifying your enemy. We know that our real enemy is not our spouse, our children, the other man or woman, the supervisor at our jobs, or any other person. Our enemies are supernatural and they are the forces of evil. We have learned that in order to have victory over our enemy, we have to be prepared to stand daily and at all times clothing ourselves in the full armor of God. The full armor includes the helmet of salvation, the breastplate of righteousness, the belt of truth, the shoes of the Gospel of peace, the sword of the Spirit, and the shield of faith."

Martin opened his Bible which caused the rest of us to do the same. "After Paul provides a detailed list of the spiritual armor needed, he then gives us some final instructions. Let's look at Ephesians 6:18. It says, 'Pray at all times, on every occasion, in every season, in the Spirit, with all manner of prayer and entreaty. To that end keep alert and watch with strong purpose and perseverance, interceding in behalf of all the saints, God's consecrated people.' His advice is to pray at all times in the Spirit and keep alert."

Martin put down his Bible and scanned the group, making eye contact with each of us. "Essentially what the apostle is telling us is that we cannot give up, give in, get tired, take a break, get lazy, get sidetracked, or anything else. Unlike football, there isn't a fourth quarter with a clock and a referee saying, 'Game over.' We have to keep fighting until this life is over or God takes the enemy out in the final battle. If we want to preserve our marriages, we have to keep praying and keep on the lookout. The minute we start thinking that everything is cool and we can just chill, the enemy will hit us with a surprise attack, and we will be laid out on the ground wondering what happened. It's sort of just like children. You know how kids are typically loud and when you can hear them, you know they're okay. But the minute everything gets quiet, especially when it comes to kids, you get nervous. Parents know that quiet means trouble. When children get quiet, unless they're sleeping, they are more than likely up to no good. The enemy is the same way. If things get too quiet and you don't see evil trying to get at you, it means one of two things—either he's already got you and you're so far in the wrong direction that he's no longer worried about you, or he's preparing for a sneak attack so get ready."

I nodded. He was right. The enemy was tricky. Although my wife and I were in a great place today, at any moment another problem could come in and attempt to break us down again. We needed to stay ready and aware.

"You all know that my wife and I love to use sayings and adages to bring home our points, so I'm going to end our final lesson with one more," Martin said. "From time to time, I hear people use the saying 'don't sleep.' Often they extend the saying to refer to themselves, such as, 'Don't sleep on me.' Saying don't sleep on me means not to underestimate the person or not to think the person is less than they really are. If you 'sleep' on a person, you might miss out on their importance or their next important move. Today, I leave you with the saying 'don't sleep' as a way of considering your enemy. Don't sleep on the enemy. Don't underestimate his tricks and plans to steal, kill, and destroy you. Stay alert and watchful. Keep praying for yourself, your spouse, you family, your friends, and others. Don't miss out on the next attack because you weren't paying attention. When Jesus was in the Garden of Gethsemane before He was arrested, he told His disciples to watch and pray. They kept falling asleep. They slept on the enemy who was preparing for probably the most infamous attack in history, the crucifixion of Jesus. Thank God that Jesus never slept. He watched, remained alert, and prayed. What pitfalls might you avoid if you watched and prayed? What attacks might you overcome if you remained alert? Don't just put on the whole armor of God, use it. Be ready in all seasons because attacks don't come at your convenience, they come when you're most vulnerable. Don't give the enemy an easy target. Don't sleep on evil."

Lesson 22: A Time to Heal

A time to kill, and a time to heal; a time to break down, and a time to build up. (Ecclesiastes 3:3)

If My people, who are called by My name, shall humble themselves, pray, seek, crave, and require of necessity My face and turn from their wicked ways, then I will hear from heaven, forgive their sin, and heal their land. (II Chronicles 7:14)

Amber

I was glowing and I knew it. But what woman wouldn't glow after a night filled with undefiled, passionate, selfless, lovemaking with her husband? And the beauty was that it didn't hurt, not one bit. I was a little nervous, but the peace of God filled me before I left that bathroom, and I knew then that it was going to be a heavenly experience.

After our session that day, I let Eric take a nap as Kelly and I went shopping on Collins Avenue where there were great stores like Guess, Express, Armani Exchange, and Banana Republic. I couldn't believe that I was hanging solo with Kelly, but she loved to shop and so did I so it worked for us. While we were out, I told Kelly that I wanted to buy something special to wear for Eric that night. I knew Kelly thought she was a hot girl, so she could lead me in the right direction. We headed over to Victoria's Secret and

I came out of there with enough lingerie to keep Eric happy for a good month.

I hid what I bought from Eric, so he had no clue what I was up to. We were down to our last nights in South Beach and I wanted them to be memorable. That night, as we prepared for bed, I made sure to be the last one in the bathroom. I showered, picked out a teddy to wear, fixed my hair, and dabbed myself with a perfume I had picked up from Vicky's. I said a quick prayer to God, asking Him to heal my body and allow our intimacy to be the beautiful experience that He created it to be.

When I opened the bathroom door, I thought Eric was going to pass out. I'd missed seeing the delight in his eyes when he was allowed to see parts of me that no other man had access to.

"You like?" I asked him. He looked like a deer caught in headlights as he responded only with a nod. I laughed.

I knew that I only needed to say three words, and that he would understand my wants and needs. So I said them, "Eric, I'm ready."

On Friday, both he and I were on cloud nine. I was elated that God had healed me from my discomfort during sex. I could finally, once again, give myself to my husband without the fear of pain. By the time we got to counseling, I was on pins and needles. I couldn't wait to tell Dr. Wilson what we had done. I guess we both must have had goofy looks on our faces because she said, "Let me guess. You two had sex."

Eric and I broke out into laughter, nodding our heads at the same time.

Dr. Wilson joined in on the joke and laughed as well. "So?" she asked me, more like a close girlfriend than a psychologist.

"No pain," I gloated.

She high fived me and we began to laugh again. "Eric?' she asked, turning his attention to him.

He beamed. "No words. It was a blessing. A true blessing."

We all agreed.

Lesson 23: A Time for Peace

A time to love, and a time to hate; a time of war, and a time of peace. (Ecclesiastes 3:8)

Finally, brethren, farewell. Be restored, be of good comfort, be of one mind, live in peace; and the God of love and peace shall be with you. (II Corinthians 13:11)

Dr. Wilson

Lem slept over last night. I felt like I was a teenager again and we were sneaking and hiding behind our parents' backs. But after a romantic night, we didn't want to be apart. He laid and talked with me for what was supposed to be a few minutes. The next thing I knew, we had both drifted to sleep. When we awoke the next morning, we agreed that he would check out of the other hotel and that we would spend our last night on South Beach in *our* hotel room together.

At the end of the final couples' class, Martin called me and Lem up to the front to give our testimony. I allowed Lem to tell his side of the story first—a tale of a home builder who forgot to properly build his own home while he was steadily building the homes of others. I listened to my husband in awe. He definitely had a gift of leadership and exhortation. When it was my turn, I told my side of the story—one of the dangers of perfection and pretense. By the time we finished with our testimony, the entire group was praising God and celebrating with us. Lydia and Martin had been right. Our story brought the spiritual battle against marriage close to home, and gave the couples a real life example of the power of faith and love.

My final sessions were sad because I had developed a connection to each of the couples that was far greater than a psychologist and her clients. I loved each of them and I would be praying for their marriages when I returned to New York. After the five sessions, I walked down to my favorite spot on the beach under that abandoned umbrella, closed my eyes, and remembered the five couples that had forever changed my life in only one week.

Eric and Amber. They had sex! I knew it from the moment I saw them at sunrise prayer that they were just a little too happy-go-lucky at 6:30 in the morning. My heart went out to them. I would always remember the couple who wanted a baby, but needed healing. I started praying that God would bless them with the desires of their heart, and that I would get an invitation to a baby shower in the near future.

Carl and Kelly. They were a riot. The Bradfords gave me hope that no couple could be counted out. Sometimes couples came to a point in their marriages when like dislike seemed greater than the like. But what these two taught me was that strong negative emotions were really just a cover up for the equally strong positive ones. Once the hardships had been washed away, they were able to love again, maybe even better than they had ever loved before.

Franklin and Tamela. They were here for someone else—for the Wilsons. For the final session, the Days left Lem in our room on the third floor, and they came to counseling alone. The Days helped me to understand that not everyone wants something from us. Some people are in our lives to give something to us. Although the Days had some minor issues that were discussed in counseling, their true purpose for being on the trip was to be used as vessels for reconciliation in my marriage. God was awesome like that. He would use whoever, whenever, to reveal His glory.

Jordan and Sarah. They needed more. Each couple has varying levels of needs. Some marriages have basic relationship issues that can be resolved in marriage therapy if both parties are willing to show up and work hard. But there are some cases when other issues like mental health are at the root of a couples' struggles. In those times, additional assistance is required. I gave my contact information to the Larks and would make it my mission to ensure they received the further help they needed when they returned back home.

Martin and Lydia. They had more life to live and love to give. Change is often hard, and as people we don't always like to let go when seasons end, but with each new phase in life, God has something wonderful in store—that future with a hope. Once the Martins stopped focusing on what they lost when their children went away to college, they began to realize the new plan God had for their lives. And what a great plan it was!

I opened my eyes for the final time, sitting on SoBe, replaying therapy sessions. It had been a good week, a really good week. I stood up and dusted the sand off my legs. Lem was back at the hotel room waiting for me. We had a dinner cruise to attend, so I needed to get back to the hotel, shower, and change. I glanced back at the abandoned umbrella that had become my place of solace during the retreat. I would miss sitting under it. I whispered goodbye to the faithful object and began my exodus from the beach, wondering when, if ever, we would meet again.

Lesson 24: A Time to Dance

A time to weep, and a time to laugh; a time to mourn, and a time
to dance. (Ecclesiastes 3:4)

Thou hast turned for me my mourning into dancing: thou hast
put off my sackcloth, and girded me with gladness.
(Psalm 30:11)

Amber

The final evening of the marriage retreat included a private
dinner cruise aboard a swanky yacht. Martin was friends with
the owner of the boat, and was able to arrange the group outing
without it costing the group a great deal of money. Everyone
dressed in their Sunday's best for an evening of rededication,
dinner, and dancing.

We all boarded the boat together at 7:00 p.m. By 7:30, we had
left the dock, and were travelling further into the Atlantic Ocean,
leaving Miami Beach behind. Most of us remained outside on the
deck, enjoying the cool breeze and darkness that surrounded us
as the boat headed away from the mainland. I stood, leaning
against the side rail, as Eric wrapped his arms around me and
shared the peaceful moment with me. I was so glad that we had
taken this adventure. Although the marriage retreat had been

filled with many conflicting emotions, we had once again weathered a major storm in our relationship, and with God's help, had come out alive. We had survived.

At 8:00 p.m., we were all gathered together at the dining area inside the boat. Six tables each with two place settings had been prepared in the area, each positioned around a small, wooden dance floor. Table tents with the last name of each couple rested atop of the tables, directing us where to sit. A few minutes after we were all seated, a man dressed in a pastoral robe entered the room and stood in the center of the dance floor.

"I greet you in the name of our Lord and Savior Jesus Christ. My name is Pastor Greg Sanders, and I am the senior pastor of Greater Grace Christian Center here in Miami, Florida. I have been asked by my good friends Pastor Franklin and Tamela Day to preside over your recommitment service tonight. I hear that you all have had a full week of activities during this marriage retreat, and that each of you have been challenged to fight the good fight of faith for your marriages.

"What will happen tonight is each of you will be called to stand with your partner and recommit yourself to your marriage. All of us will serve as witnesses. This ceremony is somewhat similar to a vow renewal without all of the distraction of guests and planning. Our goal here tonight is to remember the promise you made to both God and your spouse when you first wed. It's sort of like on New Year's Day, how we clean the slate and leave anything negative behind. When you all leave Florida and return to your homes, we want you to once again feel like newlyweds, free from the burden of past mistakes and hopeful for a promising future with your spouse."

He continued on to pray for the group and give each of us a chance to raise our hands if we were not interested in participating. No one moved, so he then went on to call each couple up in alphabetical order. Carl and Kelly Bradford were up first. It was wonderful to see them finally getting along again and how much they had developed over the retreat. Kelly had become a bit more tolerable to me over the last couple of days. I even planned to exchange cell phone numbers with her to hang out every once and a while. It would be good for the both of us—she needed more married women to hang around that would edify her and I needed to relax and have fun more often. Carl was such a jokester that during his pledge he started coughing as if he couldn't recommit himself to Kelly. She popped him lightly in the head and everyone broke out into laughter including the preacher. He redeemed himself when he planted the juiciest, more sincere kiss on her lips following their pledges. I almost cried.

Pastor Day and his wife were called second. Eric and I followed them. The order then went Jordan and Sarah, Lem and Dr. Wilson, and finally Martin and Lydia.

When I stood before the group with Eric to my right and Pastor Sanders in front of me, I felt as if I were transported back to my wedding day. Tears filled my eyes as I considered spending the rest of my life with a man that I knew loved me just as I was. I said my pledge to Eric with peace, joy, and love overflowing from my heart. At that moment, I knew that we would always choose each other no matter how rough the road became. But as the Woods had taught us during this retreat, we would have to be prepared to fight every day, and stand together for our marriage, equipped with the complete armor of God, having done all to stand against our true enemy.

I felt whole as I repeated the final words of the pledge, "I choose you today and every day for the rest of my life. What God has joined together, let no man put asunder."

Dr. Wilson

Watching each couple recommit themselves to their marriage was like watching the children I never had graduate from high school. I was proud of all of them. They had worked hard over the course of this week and now we all were experiencing the fruits of the harvest. I would have liked to believe that I had played a small role in their progress, but I couldn't give credit to anyone but God. My life had been a train wreck all week long, and it was nobody but Him who ushered each one of the couples—including Lem and I—to a place of restoration, sometimes with my help, but most times without it.

For so long, I had prided myself for being a marriage therapist, someone with the tools to help others maintain their vows. God had given me success in the field, and with His blessing, I had assisted many couples along the way. But in the process, I had taken on a role that I was never meant to play, the perfect psychologist. I wanted people to respect me and trust me with their problems so I built myself up to appear as if my life and relationship were error free. I was so afraid that if others knew that I struggled in my marriage as well that they would think I was a failure, and even more so, I would also believe the same.

Well, this week I had to face my biggest fears, issues that I thought I would never overcome. Two of the most important aspects of my life were in jeopardy, but to my surprise, God allowed it to free me from a weight that I had carried for way too long. I was now released to be myself which was an even better vessel for God to use. Married people who were in crisis didn't need a perfect psychologist with all of the right answers. They needed someone who had been through enough problems who could with confidence point them in the direction of the real Problem Solver. A good marriage wasn't about perfection, it was about letting God perfect us as we submitted our lives to Him and each other.

During our pledges, I squeezed Lem's hand and looked up at him with newfound respect and adoration. He was a mess in more ways than one, but I appreciated a little messiness in my life. It kept me grounded and aware of what really mattered. If we never paid off my car or the mortgage or any of our other bills, oh well. I didn't marry Lem to pay off bills. I married him to experience love, devotion, and companionship, and in these areas, he rarely disappointed.

After the ceremony portion of the evening ended, dinner was served, along with a surprise miniature wedding cake cutting for each couple. I looked over at Carl and Kelly who had—of course—smeared cake in each other's faces. I shook my head. Kids.

Eric also noticed the cake war happening between Carl and Kelly, but when he deviously glanced at Amber, I saw her scowl at him and mouth the words, "I wish you would!" He laughed, put down his slice of cake, and kissed her instead.

During dessert, Lydia and Martin made their way over to our table. Lem and I stood up to acknowledge them with hugs of appreciation.

"Thank you both so much for coming and helping us with this retreat," Lydia said. "The counseling sessions were great, Dr. Wilson, and I believe everyone benefited from them."

"You're welcome, but honestly, I don't know how much I helped anyone. My life was crazy this week. I feel like I should be thanking you instead," I said.

"You were just what this retreat needed," Martin replied. "It shows us all that even the most prepared of us will still face difficulties, but God's grace and mercy can still turn our troubles into triumphs. We know that it was predestined for you to be with us this week. We couldn't have picked a better person."

I sighed in relief. "Thank you both for everything." They hugged us again. God's grace was truly amazing.

Eric

Just when I thought the evening couldn't get any better, a DJ took over the turntables and switched the music from jazz to upbeat contemporary Christian music.

"Alllllll yeahhhhh, party peopleeee!" the DJ sang into the microphone. "Now it's time to get out on the floor and get your praise on!"

I heard the intro to Kirk Franklin's "This Is It" from his album *Fight of My Life* and smiled to myself. What an appropriate song. I jumped up out of my seat, grabbed Amber's hand, and led her to the center of the floor. No one else had started dancing yet, but I didn't care. I was with the woman that I loved and it was truly time to dance in celebration. Amber looked at me apprehensively at first, then shrugged and joined in with me dipping from side to side.

Carl, who swore he was Mr. Soul Train himself, leaped up and ran onto the dance floor with Kelly almost beating him there. He wrapped his left arm around her waist, pulled her close, then kissed her on the cheek before releasing her, and allowing her to break out into some version of the Harlem Shake. Carl started Pop-Locking and doing the Robot, and Amber and I fell out laughing. Quickly, others joined us on the dance floor until everyone in the room was dancing and singing along, telling the devil that he no longer had control over our lives.

As the dinner cruise, the evening, and the marriage retreat came to an end, I felt for the first time in a long time a glimmer of expectancy in my spirit. I didn't know if it was the recommitment of our vows or the fact that Amber and I had finally made love again—pain free—but something, I suspect it was the voice of God, let me know that more miracles were on the way.

Epilogue - One Year Later
Lesson 25: A Time to Be Born

A time to be born, and a time to die; a time to plant, and a time to pluck up that which is planted. (Ecclesiastes 3:2)

A woman when she is in travail hath sorrow, because her hour is come: but as soon as she is delivered of the child, she remembereth no more the anguish, for joy that a man is born into the world. (John 16:21)

Dr. Wilson

I hung up the phone. I couldn't believe what I had just heard. I sat in shock for seven or eight minutes until Lem entered the kitchen, said my name, and shook me out of my daze.

"Who was that?" he asked as he pour himself a cup of coffee. It was a little after 9:00 a.m. on a Monday, and we rarely received calls that early unless it was an emergency.

"That was my editor from the publishing house. My book landed on the New York Times Bestsellers List. It's number seven in nonfiction."

"That's wonderful, sweetheart!" he exclaimed as he grabbed me up in his arms, hugged, and kissed me.

I was still numb, but I returned his affection and celebrated with him.

Following the couples' retreat, I decided to step back a bit from counseling and to put more energy into my own family. I still continued to do speaking engagements and a few retreats, but I closed down my counseling office and referred my existing clients to other marriage therapist that I trusted. Spending more time at home allowed me to work on a few books that I had been tossing around my brain for years. One particular book, titled *The Not So Perfect Marriage,* examined people's ideals of marriage and how these preconceptions actually keep marriages from being what couples truly desired. I sat down in December to write it and the words seemed to pour out of me as if I was always meant to write them. By late January, a friend of mine, who is also a literary agent and had been begging me to write a book, began shopping the book idea around to various publishers she had relationships with. In record time, I had a book deal that was too good to refuse from a publisher who was seeking high quality nonfiction books. It all happened so fast and unbelievably easy that I kept waiting for the other shoe to drop, and for a harsh dose of reality to smack me in my face. It never happened. The book had been released only a few weeks prior and was flying off the shelves. Me being somewhat of a well-known psychologist, as well as doing a few big time, national TV interviews before the release had created a major buzz about the book. People were dying to get their hands on it.

I laughed at the humor of it all. I knew why people really wanted the book. Inside its pages, I told my true story of how I almost single-handedly ruined my own marriage while I was conducting marriage counseling at a couples' retreat. The world was waiting to hear about the imperfect psychologist who couldn't live up to her own advice. It was amazing how God took my biggest fear, my flaws being exposed to the public, and made it my biggest success. All I had to do was submit myself to Him and His way of doing things.

Since the retreat, Lem had also made some changes including handling his business affairs in a more professional manner. He now made sure that deposits were made before he started any job, and that he was paid in full before he finished it. The company that owed him the $20,000 ended up paying him a month and a half after the retreat. He honored his commitment to me and repaid me for the borrowed money for the mortgage and his car note, and paid off my car loan. He also gave me a surprising $1,000 instead of the $500 extra he had promised. And he took me to Niagara Falls for a date night filled with dinner, dancing, and a pair of new diamond earrings. Like I said, breaking up was never fun, the making up part was so rewarding.

With the news of my successful book, I felt overwhelmed with appreciation. I backed away from my husband's arms and said, "Thank you, baby, for loving me, flaws and all."

He smiled at me and pulled me close to him again. "I never wanted a perfect wife anyway. I just wanted you." He kissed me on my forehead. Being inside the safety of Lem's arms felt better than all of the accolades career success could ever give me.

I tipped my head upwards to see his face. "So, now that I'm a New York Times bestselling author, I think we should talk about having kids."

He released me from his arms and returned to his coffee which was cooling on the countertop. "I don't know. I'm still not financially stable."

I frowned at him. "Look, man. I'm not Sarah from the Bible. I can't have babies at 300-years-old."

He started checking his pants pockets and looking around frantically. "Is that my phone ringing?"

"Come on, babe! At least can we get a cat? A rooster? A pet kangaroo? Something?" I whined.

He chuckled and approached me from behind, wrapping his arms around my waist. "Woman, you know I'm just messing with you. Whenever you're ready, we can have as many children as you want. But I'm telling you right now. I come from a long line of baby-making men. I've been holding back on you, but once I let it all out, you might end up like that Octomom chick with babies everywhere."

I laughed. "Oh really? I'm not scared. If you think you're bad, bring it on!"

He looked around suspiciously, then said, "Last one to the bedroom is a rotten egg."

I took off up the stairs, but he gained on me and gently tugged on my left ankle, bringing me stomach down on the stairs. Taking advantage of my fall, he sprang up the stairs ahead of me. Not to be outdone, I picked myself up and chased him down the hallway, tackling him as he entered the bedroom, both of us crashing to the floor. Our laughter filled the room.

He kissed me on my cheek and said, "You sure you want to have children? Between you and I, there may already be enough kids in this house."

I giggled. "You just might have a point. But let's have a kid or two anyways. I may need some new material for my next book."

Amber

On November 1st at 11:30 a.m., Eric Hayes Jr. entered the world.

Following the marriage retreat, Eric and I decided that we would have faith in God and stop trying to control our own destiny. If it was for us to have a baby together, we would—in His time. If not, we would be grateful for the blessing of my stepdaughter, Jonelle, and the opportunity to give her unconditional love.

We began enjoying intimacy again, not just sex, but being close to each other through mutual respect, love, and appreciation. Dr. Wilson had been right; the minute I unchained myself from the hidden pain, guilt, and resentment, sex became enjoyable and beautiful. I was free to trust Eric again with my body, and in return, receive the blessing of motherhood.

When we found out that I was pregnant again, we agreed to take the process one day at a time and hope for the best. My doctor monitored me closely, making sure that my blood pressure remained normal throughout the pregnancy. As my due date drew closer, the stress on my body begin to take a toll on me, and it was decided that I would be scheduled for a cesarean rather than hold out for natural childbirth. I was given a few medications to ensure that the baby would be fully developed since they would have to deliver the baby prematurely. My family, friends, and church prayed earnestly for my safety, and that of my unborn child.

Almost two years after my first miscarriage, God granted my request for a child, and I met my miracle face to face. I knew that it was a blessing because although I was able to finally conceive, many other wonderful women who desired children were unable to do so. I met many of them along the way to my journey of becoming a mother, and I promised God that I would not forget them now that I had received my gift.

To those women, I offer encouragement. God has not forgotten you, and He loves you dearly. There is a time and there is a season for everything. And if for some reason, your time and your season never comes, God's loving arms will hold you, as He held me, and as He holds us all through life's biggest disappointments. He's with you, and He still has amazing plans for you. Just wait and see.

A Note from Andrea

Writing a Christian fiction book with a strong Biblical message is not an easy task. My process of writing *Wife 101* was enjoyable for the most part, but that was because both I and the enemy had no idea what I was penning. I still remember getting those first reactions about *Wife 101* and readers telling me how great of an impact the novel had on their lives. I was shocked. Yes, I was proud of my book and I had intended it to be a tool of empowerment, but I never imagined that it would touch others the way it did.

Writing *Husband 101* was tough. I had to fight tooth and nail to finish that book. There were times when I wondered if I could really do it again. But God was faithful and the book was not only birthed, but it was effective. Those who read it, both men and women, reported gaining much needed lessons from its pages. I felt relieved and blessed.

I went into writing *Couples 101* with much more confidence that, once again, God would be with me and use me to write another powerful novel that could touch the hearts of men. Yet, once again, the fight was back and trying to finish the manuscript was exhausting. It was during this process that I realized the intense spiritual battle that was occurring each time I sat down to write a Christian book. It wasn't just me being lazy or overwhelmed—the enemy really didn't want me to get these words out to the public. Nonetheless, not writing and publishing these books is not an option, despite the obstacles. This series is meant to do more than just entertain you; it is created to equip you with many of the tools you need to be successful in your

marriages, dating relationships, and families. We all learn a
different way, using different techniques. Some of us understand
and retain information better if we can connect it to a relatable
example. The Wife 101 Series hopes to serve as that example, to
empower you and strengthen you in the best and worst of times.

There are a few special treats in *Couples 101*. First, readers get
to witness the combined perspectives of Eric and Amber Hayes.
Wife 101 was told only from the perspective of Amber, and
Husband 101 was told only from the view of Eric. In *Couples 101*,
both parties get to "weigh in" on their experience at the marriage
retreat. I pray you enjoy getting both points of view in one book.
Second, readers are given the opportunity to take a sneak peek at
the relationships of other couples at the retreat. Feedback from a
few readers of previous Wife 101 Series books indicated that there
was an interest in knowing what the other class members were
going through or thought about the courses. It would have been
too much and too distracting to give the full stories of the other
couples/class members, but via the psychologist, readers are able
to get a brief glance at the counseling sessions of the participating
marriage retreat couples, including the Woods. Third, readers get
to meet a new main character, Dr. Andrea Wilson. Over the course
of *Wife 101* and *Husband 101*, I've had many readers ask me if I
was either Lydia or Amber (if these characters were based off my
life or personality). I am neither, and honestly, I'm not even the
character in *Couples 101* who's my namesake. But I thought it
would be interesting (and a bit challenging) to add a character
with my name to the book to provide the mental health aspect of
the story. To my surprise, the character began to do her own thing
and ran away with the story, significantly adding to an already
conflict-filled plot. Writing the Dr. Wilson character was actually
fun, and hopefully, you will enjoy meeting her.

I thank God for every person who has taken this journey of
faith with me. To every family member, friend, colleague, reader,
book club, literary professional, reviewer, editor, and angel who

has taken the time to support me and/or this series, I am extremely grateful. Continue with me to trust God, stand for what is righteous, and press toward the mark which is the higher calling of God through Christ Jesus.

Happy Reading,

Andrea J. Wilson

Reading Group Guide

1. In Couples 101, there were six couples participating in a marriage retreat. Which couple was your favorite? Which could you relate to most? Why?

2. The retreat was held in South Beach, Miami, Florida, which is an unusual marriage retreat location. What did you think about the Woods deciding to throw these couples into "the lion's den?"

3. The Couples 101 classes focused on Ephesians 6:11-18 (the full armor of God). Which of these lessons did you enjoy most? Why?

4. The alternating lessons in the book focused on Ecclesiastes 3:1-8 (a time for everything). Which of these lessons did you enjoy most? Why?

5. Eric and Amber struggle with reproductive issues which affect their intimacy level as a married couple. Discuss the reality of their situation and how reproduction issues can impact a marriage.

6. Amber's harbored resentment about her miscarriages caused a physical ailment (painful intercourse). Do you believe that physical illness can result from psychological problems (called psychosomatic issues)? Discuss how psychological and sexual issues can impact a marriage.

7. Dr. Wilson is hired to provide therapy for the couples at the marriage retreat, and surprisingly finds her own marriage at risk. Discuss your perception of

people in the helping role and your expectations of their lives and relationships. Do you expect marriage counselors to have close-to-perfect marriages? Does marital status, age, or marriage condition impact your willingness to receive support from someone related to relationships/marriage?

8. Lem uses money from his joint account with Andrea to pay his employees for a job. Discuss his decision and his wife's reaction to his decision.

9. Carl and Kelly deal with the issue of a mid-life crisis, Martin and Lydia face empty nest syndrome, Franklin and Tamela address end of life issues, and Jordan and Sarah present PTSD and communication problems. Discuss the various counseling issues of the supporting characters and whether or not you think these problems exist in real life marriages.

10. Was there anything that surprised you in the book or anything you would change about the outcome of the book? What do foresee happening next in the lives of Eric and Amber Hayes?

*For more questions related to Couples 101 or to relate the lessons in the novel to your personal experiences, please check out The Couples 101 Workbook at www.amazon.com/author/andreawilson

Recommended Resources

Relationship Development
Kiss & Tell: Releasing Expectations by A'ndrea J. Wilson, Ph.D.
The Power of a Praying Wife by Stormie Omartian
The Power of a Praying Husband by Stormie Omartian
The Power of Praying Together by Stormie Omartian
The Five Love Languages by Gary Chapman

Spiritual Warfare
A Divine Revelation of Spiritual Warfare by Mary Baxter and Dr.
T. L. Lowery

Communication Skills Training
Couples Communication/The Awareness Wheel
(www.couplescommunication.com)

Wife 101

The Wife 101 Series, Book #1

Final Exam Question #1

Is an independent woman destined to remain single forever or can a wife training course turn a mess into a Mrs.?

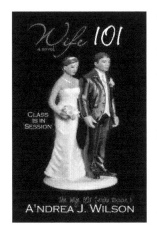

Thriving Atlanta mogul Amber Ross thinks she is the perfect woman. But when she finds out that her recent ex-boyfriend is marrying someone else, she begins to question what men really want. Frustrated with the dating scene and her failing interactions with men, Amber enrolls in a course at her church geared towards teaching women how to be effective in their relationships: Wife 101. Amber expects the class to shed some light on her courting flaws, but it does more than that; it challenges many of her life choices and ideas about romance. Her new attitude brings unexpected love, but has she learned enough to make the right choices and snag a great husband, or like a foolish woman, will she tear down her home with her own hands?

Husband 101

The Wife 101 Series, Book #2

Final Exam Question #2

How many women does it take to ruin a marriage?

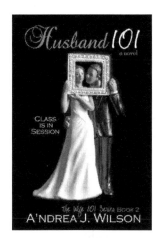

Eric Hayes is a man with too many women in his life. As a bachelor, he loved all of the attention, but now being a married man, he quickly realizes that he cannot please more than one woman at a time. Succumbing to the pressure, Eric takes a course at his wife's church to become better equipped for the bittersweet realities of marriage: Husband 101. The course ends up being more than he bargained for and his role and actions as a man are put to the test, one that he struggles to pass. Unable to keep everyone satisfied, Eric's picture-perfect life begins to crumble even before he can make it to his first anniversary. Will he heed to good advice and put into practice the lessons that can salvage his family, or will pride and self-reliance guarantee his fall?

The **Wife** 101 Workbook
The **Husband** 101 Workbook
The **Couples** 101 Workbook

Experience the novels Wife 101, Husband 101, and Couples 101 firsthand with The Wife 101 Workbook. The Husband 101 Workbook, and The Couples 101 Workbook. These interactive study guides by Author and Marriage & Family Educator, Dr. A'ndrea J. Wilson, take readers beyond the novel and into the actual 101 courses. Take a deeper look inside the lessons of each book, and the classes that make the Wife 101 Series unforgettable novels. Follow along as Amber, Eric, and their classmates are challenged to become better interpersonally and intrapersonally. Get a richer understanding of the role of men and woman, and how the Word of God directs us to think and behave. Use these workbooks along with the novels as a part of your church group, book club, or in your personal quiet time.

Available now at Amazon.com and Divinegardenpress.com

Divine Garden Press Introduces

Janell

Thrillers for the Soul

www.iamjanell.com

Divine Garden Press

...redeeming marriages and families one book at a time.

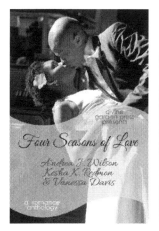

WWW.DIVINEGARDENPRESS.COM

A'ndrea J. Wilson, Ph.D. is the bestselling author of both fiction and nonfiction books, including the novels, *Wife 101* & *Husband 101,* and the devotional, *My Business His Way: Wisdom & Inspiration for Entrepreneurs.* She holds a Bachelor's of Science in Psychology, a Master's of Science in Counseling Psychology; Marriage and Family Therapy, and a Doctorate in Global Leadership; Educational Leadership. A'ndrea works as a college professor, as well as conducts workshops on a variety of personal and professional topics. Dr. Wilson is the Founder and President of Divine Garden Press, a publishing company that specializes in books addressing marriage and family issues. A native of Rochester, New York, she currently resides in Georgia. Please visit her online at www.andreawilsononline.com and www.wife101.com or email her at drajwilson@gmail.com.

Other Books by A'ndrea J. Wilson

Nonfiction

My Business His Way: Wisdom & Inspiration for Entrepreneurs

Kiss & Tell: Releasing Expectations

The Wife 101/Husband 101/Couples 101 Workbooks

Fiction

Husband 101

Wife 101

Ready & Able Teens: Ebony's Bad Habit

Ready & ABLE Teens: Desiree Dishes the Dirt

As Janell

Spell

Spell 2: Empty Vessels (March 2014)

Made in the USA
Columbia, SC
24 May 2022